Surprises According to Humphrey

Betty G. Birney has written episodes for many children's television shows and is the author of over twenty-five books. Her work has won many awards, including an Emmy and three Humanitas Prizes. Betty's first book about Humphrey, *The World According to Humphrey*, won Richard and Judy's Children's Books prize in the 7+ age category. *Adventure According to Humphrey* was written specially for World Book Day. She lives in America with her husband.

Join Humphrey on more of his adventures!

·'ö'·

The World According to Humphrey
Friendship According to Humphrey
Adventure According to Humphrey
(special publication for World Book Day)
Trouble According to Humphrey

·'ö'·

Praise for *The World According to Humphrey*:

'Humphrey, a delightful, irresistible character, is
big hearted, observant and creative, and his
experiences . . . range from comedic to touching.'
Booklist

'This read is simply good-good-good.' *Kirkus
Reviews*

'Breezy, well-crafted first novel.' *Publishers Weekly*

·'ö'·

Praise for *Friendship According to Humphrey*:

'An effective exploration of the joys and pains of
making and keeping friends, which will strike a
chord with many children.' *Telegraph*

SURPRISES ACCORDING TO HUMPHREY

Betty G. Birney

faber and faber

First published in 2008
by Faber and Faber Limited
3 Queen Square London WC1N 3AU

Typeset by Faber and Faber
Printed in England by CPI Bookmarque, CR0 4TD

The right of Betty G. Birney to be
identified as author of this work has been asserted
in accordance with Section 77 of the Copyright, Designs
and Patents Act 1988

A CIP record for this book
is available from the British Library

ISBN 978–0–571–23717–3

2 4 6 8 10 9 7 5 3

Contents

1 Spring has Sprung . . . 1

2 Stop, Drop and More Surprises . . . 14

3 Hamster on a Roll . . . 21

4 Spring Fever . . . 31

5 Surprise from Outer Space . . . 40

6 The Space Alien Sqeaks . . . 50

7 Surprise Attack . . . 62

8 The Hunt Continues . . . 73

9 No Surprises . . . 83

10 The Return of Mi Amigo . . . 94

11 Hoppin' with Heidi . . . 102

12 Testing . . . Testing . . . 112

13 The Big Break . . . 124

14 A Day at Maycrest Manor . . . 133

15 Suggestions and Surprises . . . 140

Humphrey's Top Ten Good
    Surprises . . . 153

Spring has Sprung

Monday mornings are different from other mornings.

That's just one of many things I've learned in the months I've lived in Room 26 of Longfellow School.

For one thing, on Mondays, I'm usually tired from a weekend spent visiting the home of one of my classmates. That's the BEST-BEST-BEST part of my job as classroom hamster.

My friends are also quieter than usual on Mondays. It takes them at least a half a day to get back up to speed after their weekends away from school.

Don't-Complain-Mandy Payne complains more than usual on Monday. Today she complained that it was too hot. Our teacher, Mrs Brisbane, opened a window.

Sit-Still-Seth Stevenson jitters in his seat more

on Monday mornings. But he tries to sit still – he really does.

And even Lower-Your-Voice-A.J., who can rattle the walls with his loud voice, is quieter on Monday mornings. It's weird.

Mrs Brisbane, however, is always up to speed, and she likes to get Monday mornings rolling with something interesting.

'Class, in case you hadn't noticed, spring has sprung!' Mrs Brisbane announced one Monday.

I don't know about the other students, but I'd certainly noticed that the March rains had stopped and everything had changed. The world, which had been drippy and dreary, was now bright green. The trees, the grass – just about everything outside – matched the colour of my goofy green neighbour, Og the Frog, who lives in a tank next to my cage.

For some reason, all that green made me feel like springing up onto my bridge ladder, which goes across my big cage.

Mrs Brisbane kept talking. 'And today, I have a special spring surprise for you!'

Surprise? Surprises are fun, like birthday presents. But surprises can be not-so-fun, like unexpected storms with LOUD-LOUD-LOUD thunder that can hurt the ears of small, sensitive creatures like me. Just thinking about thunder made me bobble, then wobble. I tried to catch my balance, but tumbled off my ladder with a loud 'Thump!' Luckily, I landed in a pile of soft bedding (and not in my poo corner), but still, I was very surprised and quite startled.

My neighbour Og was startled, too, I suppose, because he let out a large 'BOING!' which is the strange twanging sound that green frogs, like him, usually make.

'What's going on over here?' Mrs Brisbane walked towards the table by the window where Og and I live.

'Humphrey fell! I saw him!' a voice called out. Even though I couldn't see who was talking from underneath all that bedding, I knew it was Raise-Your-Hand-Heidi Hopper, because no matter how many times she'd been told, Heidi never remembered to raise her hand.

'Hands, please, Heidi,' Mrs Brisbane reminded her.

I poked my head out of the bedding and saw her looking down at me. 'Are you all right, Humphrey?'

'I'm not hurt,' I explained. 'But I am a bit shaken up.'

As usual, all that came out was 'SQUEAK-SQUEAK-SQUEAK.'

'He certainly sounds fine,' said Mrs Brisbane. 'Now, back to our surprise.'

I stood up to give her my full attention.

'I've been working you pretty hard on our pre-test exercises,' she continued.

That was certainly true. We had tests from time to time in Room 26. But there were *bigger* tests coming and Mrs Brisbane wanted to make sure her students did well. There were maths exercises and reading exercises and her favourite: the dictionary exercise. Every day, she had a list of words for us to look up in the dictionary. Then we were supposed to write sentences using the words correctly.

There was just one problem: everyone in class had a dictionary except me! This was very annoying to me, because I try to keep up with my friends. Finally, I came up with a solution and made my own dictionary by writing words and definitions in the tiny notebook I keep hidden in my cage. Ms Mac, the wonderful supply teacher who brought me to Room 26, gave it to me. (She also gave me a broken heart when she left to teach in faraway Brazil. I still think about Ms Mac a lot.)

Now Mrs Brisbane was smiling broadly. 'This morning, we're taking a break from exercises to decorate the room.'

My classmates cheered.

'What did she say?' Pay-Attention-Art Patel asked Lower-Your-Voice-A.J.

'No test exercises!' A.J. bellowed loudly.

That got Stop-Giggling-Gail Morgenstern chuckling and her best friend, Heidi, joined in.

Mrs Brisbane shushed everyone. 'Settle down now. The theme of the day is Spring into Numbers. Now, let's get to work!'

None of us knew what she was talking about, but soon, all my friends were busy with paper, paint, markers, cotton wool, string and wire. How I wished I could get my paws on some of those things!

While Mrs Brisbane explained that the students were supposed to hide maths problems in their flower, tree and kite projects, I scurried to my wheel for a little exercise. Spring made me feel frisky and full of life! I spun faster and faster until the whole room was a blur. And then the break bell rang.

My classmates dropped their markers and construction paper and raced towards the door. Wait-For-The-Bell-Garth Tugwell was the first one out, as usual.

For some reason, the bell surprised me, maybe because it sounded a little softer than normal. I think it surprised Mrs Brisbane, too, because she glanced at the clock and shouted, 'Children! Come back here!' She raced to the door and called the students back. 'It's not break yet.'

I could hear them objecting.

'It was the bell!' A.J. bellowed.

'We'll miss break!' Mandy protested.

But Mrs Brisbane was firm. Once my friends were back in the room, she pointed to the clock. 'See? It's not time yet.' She checked her watch. 'Not for another half an hour.'

'But the bell rang!' Heidi argued.

'Raise-Your-Hand-Heidi,' Mrs Brisbane said, just as she's said hundreds of times before. 'Would someone like to tell me what just happened?' Mrs Brisbane's eagle eyes stared out at the classroom.

'April Fool!' a voice called out.

'I-Heard-That-Kirk Chen,' the teacher said. 'It was you, wasn't it?'

Kirk was the class comic, but he'd been better lately about playing practical jokes during school hours.

'I'm sorry, Mrs Brisbane,' Kirk answered. 'But it's April the first. April Fools' Day! You're supposed to play jokes on people.'

Mrs Brisbane asked him to explain what he did.

'Last week, I made a recording of the break bell.' He held up a TINY-TINY-TINY tape recorder. 'I just played it a little ahead of time.'

Mrs Brisbane shook her head. 'Kirk, I don't know what I'm going to do with you.'

'I didn't hurt anybody,' Kirk protested.

'No, but –'

Mrs Brisbane didn't finish, because all of a sudden the loudest sound I've ever heard rattled my furry little ears. It was much louder than the buzzers and bells that sound at morning, break, lunchtime or at the end of the day. It was louder than the loudest voice A.J. ever used. It wasn't a ringing or a buzzing – it was an ear-splitting BEEP-BEEP-BEEP without stopping.

'Help!' I squeaked, plummeting off my wheel and somersaulting through my bedding. It's never a good idea to stop spinning too quickly.

'Fire drill!' Heidi called out. She didn't raise her hand but this time Mrs Brisbane didn't scold her.

The beeps kept blaring. Couldn't someone turn them off?

'Boys and girls, it *is* the fire alarm,' Mrs Brisbane shouted. 'Leave everything on your desks. Line up row by row and we'll calmly walk out to the playground.'

'BOING-BOING!' Og sounded worried.

We hadn't had a fire drill since Og came to our classroom. No wonder he was alarmed. I quickly explained that a fire drill is a time for students to practise how to act if there's a fire. My friends knew just what to do. They put down their pencils, scissors and papers, stood up and began to form lines.

'Stay calm,' Mrs Brisbane said. I don't know how *anyone* could stay calm with that noise. 'They didn't tell me about a fire drill, so this one could be a real alarm.'

I was impressed with how orderly the students were, except for Miranda Golden, who was usually one of the best-behaved students in class. She left the line and hurried to my cage. 'Come on, Humphrey, I'll look out for you.'

Good old Miranda. I think of her as Golden Miranda, because she is an almost perfect person. And her hair is as golden as my fur.

Then Garth and A.J. broke ranks and raced over to Og. Each of them took one end of his tank to carry him.

'Children! Stop!' Mrs Brisbane shouted. 'Leave Og and Humphrey here. You must leave everything in the classroom!'

'But if it's a real fire, we can't leave them here!' Miranda protested. I do love that girl.

'Yeah, that would be awful!' A.J. agreed.

Mrs Brisbane bit her lip and looked out into the corridor. 'It's probably a surprise drill, but all right. Hurry along. And keep that tank level, please!'

I didn't know if there was a fire or not, but it felt like we were having an earthquake, because as Miranda carried my cage, I was slipping and sliding. Thank goodness for that nice soft bedding!

As my cage lurched down the corridor, I saw us head towards a side door. This was a surprise because I'd only been in and out of the school through the main entrance before. Suddenly, I felt fresh spring air on my fur and there was BRIGHT-BRIGHT-BRIGHT light in my eyes. I couldn't smell any smoke, and best of all, the awful beeping stopped.

'It's okay, Humphrey,' Miranda told me. 'We're out on the playground.'

The playground? The playground! The place where my classmates went every day, but where I had never been before. I took a chance and stood up to look around. I saw swings, a slide, a tall something-or-other with rings hanging down from it. It was almost as cool as my cage, with its wheel, ladders and tree branches.

And there were students and teachers from other classes standing around. There was Small-Paul Fletcher, who was in Mrs Loomis's class, but came into Room 26 for maths every morning. He didn't look so small compared to the other students in his class.

Wow, I'd never seen that tall teacher with the bright red hair. Or the teacher who looked a bit like Father Christmas. They were all talking and laughing, so I knew it was just a practice fire after all. I was still taking it all in when – SCREECH! – the loudest whistle on earth blasted very near my cage.

'Mrs Brisbane!' a voice bellowed.

A shadow fell over my cage. I looked up and saw that the large object casting the shadow was actually a woman. A woman holding a whistle.

'You should know by now that nothing should be taken from the classroom. Nothing!' Her voice was almost as loud as her whistle, but a lot deeper.

'I know, Mrs Wright, but the children had a point. If this was a real fire, they would want to save their pets.'

'Unacceptable!' the woman called Mrs Wright declared. I braced myself in case she blew her whistle again.

'He's a living creature! A living thing!' said Miranda. Did I mention how much I love that girl?

Then I heard a familiar voice. 'What's going on here?'

'A serious breach of the rules,' Mrs Wright roared. 'Nothing must leave the classrooms except the students. Nothing!'

'And the teacher!' I added. I was a little afraid of this woman, but still, someone had to squeak up for Mrs Brisbane.

I saw Mr Morales's face smiling down at me. He's the head and also the Most Important Person at Longfellow School. As usual, he was wearing an interesting tie. This one had fluffy white clouds on a blue background.

'You mean Humphrey? And Og?' he asked.

'They're not things, Mr Morales. They're living creatures,' Miranda protested.

'And they're part of our class,' added Garth.

'Yeah!' A.J. bellowed and this time Mrs Brisbane didn't tell him to lower his voice.

Mrs Wright waved a paper in Mr Morales's face, which was RUDE-RUDE-RUDE!

'There are rules, and as Supervisor of Emergency Services, I must strongly protest,' she said. 'I'm sorry, but Mrs Brisbane has chosen to ignore the rules!'

Those were fighting words. Because nobody I knew followed the rules better than Mrs Brisbane. At least if they were good rules.

'Look, the children have a point,' she said, in a nice, soft voice (unlike Mrs Wright's loud, unpleasant voice). 'You can't expect them to leave behind their beloved pets.'

'It's up to us to enforce the rules.' Mrs Wright fingered her whistle but thank goodness, she didn't blow on it.

'Well . . .' said Mr Morales.

'If I had argued with them, it would have slowed us down,' Mrs Brisbane explained. 'That's not good in a fire.'

'BOING!' Goodness, I was surprised to hear Og squeak up, but I was glad he was on our side.

Then I heard a brand-new voice. 'That went well,' a man's voice said.

Mrs Wright shook her head. 'Not entirely. We'll have to try again before the end of the year.'

The person behind the new voice came into view. He was wearing a big shiny yellow jacket and big yellow trousers. And on his head was a COOL-COOL-COOL black hat with a big brim.

'Hi, everybody,' he said, smiling. 'I'm Jeff Herman from the fire station.'

'Did you bring the fire engine?' Garth asked.

'It's out front. You guys did a good job with the fire drill today.'

Mrs Wright shook her head. 'I'm afraid these children did not. They took the time to bring this rat and this frog outside. Strictly against the rules.'

A rat! You would think that a person who teaches in a school could tell the difference between an ordinary rat and a handsome golden hamster like me!

Firefighter Jeff pushed his hat back on his head. 'If there's a real fire, you shouldn't stop to get your pets. Your job is to get out safely. Don't go back in for anything. But tell the firefighters your pet is inside. We rescue pets from fires all the time.'

He bent down and looked me right in the eye. 'Especially nice little hamsters like this guy.'

At least one clever person could tell a hamster from a rat!

'But the best thing to learn is how to prevent a fire from happening,' he continued. 'I'll tell you about that when I visit your class later.'

WOW-WOW-WOW! A real live firefighter was coming to Room 26! Now, *that's* the kind of surprise I like.

DICTIONARY: a book giving the meanings of very cool words, how to say them and where those words came from. (Question: is the word 'dictionary' in the dictionary?)

Humphrey's Dictionary
of Wonderful Words

Stop, Drop and More Surprises

Kirk had to stay in during afternoon break and write a letter of apology on the blackboard.

Even though she pretended to be annoyed, I don't think Mrs Brisbane thought his prank was that bad. After all, it was very clever of him to think of recording the bell.

True to his word, Jeff Herman visited our classroom late in the day. He showed us pictures of very cool fire engines with noisy sirens, and he told us not to play with matches (which I've never done). Then he told us something very important: if your clothes ever catch fire, you should remember three things.

'Who knows what those three things are?' he asked.

Seth and Garth raised their hands right away but before anyone called on them, Heidi blurted out, 'Stop, drop and roll!'

'Raise-Your-Hand-Heidi Hopper, *please*!' Mrs Brisbane sounded really annoyed. 'Sorry, Mr Herman,' she told the firefighter.

He just smiled and explained that if your or a friend's clothes ever catch fire, you should stop, drop to the floor and roll. That will put out the fire. Then came the fun part. He made us all practise. My friends stood by their desks (and I stood in my cage) and shouted, 'Stop! Drop! Roll!' Then we'd drop to the ground and roll on the floor. I was luckier than my friends because I have such soft bedding on the bottom of my cage. I think even Og must have practised because I heard splashing coming from his cage.

Jeff Herman gave the students stickers that said 'Stop-Drop-Roll' and suddenly, school was over for the day. Everybody was smiling and happy except for Mrs Brisbane. She frowned as she stopped Heidi on her way out of class.

'Heidi, it's bad enough when you won't raise your hand in class, but when we have a guest and you speak out like that, it's rude and embarrassing.'

Heidi looked up at Mrs Brisbane with big sad eyes. 'I'm sorry,' she said. 'I forgot.'

'You remember to come to school and you remember to do your homework, I'm happy to say. Why can't you remember to raise your hand?'

'I suppose it's a bad habit,' Heidi explained.

Mrs Brisbane sighed loudly. 'I'd better call your parents in. Again.'

The Hoppers had already been in twice this school year and both times they said Heidi was well behaved at home. They promised to talk to her about her disruptive behaviour. Each time, Heidi was quiet for a day or two after the meeting, but she'd always gone back to blurting things out.

Mrs Brisbane dismissed Heidi so she could catch her bus. Then she slowly walked over to the table where Og and I live.

'Fellows,' she said, 'if there's one thing I want to accomplish by the end of the school year, it's getting Heidi Hopper to raise her hand.'

'If anyone can do it, you can!' I shouted, but of course all she heard was SQUEAK-SQUEAK-SQUEAK. That's the problem with being a class-room hamster. I can read, I can write and I can help my friends. But it's hard for me to make myself understood.

'Sometimes I wish I had a magic wand to wave all my students' problems away,' she said. Then she stared right at me. 'Come to think of it, Humphrey, you're not too good about raising your paw, either. See you boys tomorrow.'

After she left, I thought about what Mrs Brisbane had said. 'You know, Og, I understand Heidi's problem. I do forget to raise my paw before squeaking up in class. Of course, I wouldn't get called on anyway. But Heidi could, and she's a clever girl. She should be able to learn.'

'BOING!' I'd finally decided that the odd sound Og made was his way of agreeing with me.

'And Mrs Brisbane knows so many things, like how to get Speak-Up-Sayeh to speak up, and how to get Pay-Attention-Art to pay more attention. Surely she can find a way to help Heidi!'

Og apparently didn't have any opinion on the subject, so I crawled into my sleeping hut to think things over.

·ö·

SQUEAK-SQUEAK-SQUEAK. The sound woke me from my doze, and this time I wasn't the one squeaking. It was Aldo, coming in to clean the room. His trolley needed a little bit of oil to stop that noise.

I peeped out from my sleeping hut. The lights came on, temporarily blinding me, but I heard Aldo's familiar voice.

'¡Buenas noches, señores! ¿Como estás?'

The voice sounded like Aldo's, but for the first time ever, I couldn't understand a word he was saying. It reminded me of the weekend I spent at Sayeh's house, when I couldn't understand her family. It took me a while to realize that they were speaking another language. But Aldo had always spoken English until tonight.

'Aldo? Is that you?' I squeaked.

My eyes got used to the light and I could see that the person in the room actually was Aldo. He stopped and looked up at the clock. *'Son las siete y medio.'*

'Huh?' I squeaked.

Og let out an alarming 'BOING!' I suppose he was surprised to hear Aldo's strange new way of speaking, too.

Aldo looked puzzled. 'Or is it *media*? I always forget.' He set to work, moving the desks, sweeping the floor, dusting the desks, all the while muttering strange words, like *'Me llama Aldo. ¿Como está usted? ¿Donde está el . . . ? ¿Donde está la* – oh, mamma mia, those *el*s and *la*s – *¿Donde está la escuela?'*

He swept more and more furiously.

'Tengo un lápiz. El tiene un lápiz. Tienen . . . tienen . . . lápices.'

'Og, can you understand what he's saying?' I called over to my green, goggle-eyed friend.

'BOING-BOING!' he twanged back.

Yeah, he was just as puzzled as I was.

Aldo put the desks back in place, then pulled up a chair close to my cage and took out his lunch bag. He tore a little piece of lettuce from his sandwich and poked it through the bars of my cage. 'Here, *muchacho.'*

'Thanks!' I squeaked.

'I don't know the word for lettuce.' Aldo sounded discouraged.

What on earth was my friend talking about? The word for 'lettuce' is 'lettuce', isn't it?

Aldo ate in silence, then suddenly stood up. 'Well, gotta go, *amigos*,' he said, opening the blinds.

I remembered that Mr Morales called me *amigo*, too.

'*Hasta luego*!'

'Whatever,' I squeaked back in total confusion.

Soon, Aldo was gone, the lights were out and the room was bathed in the silvery glow of the street-light coming through the open blinds. I could hear Og swimming in his tank but I didn't pay much attention.

I was too busy thinking about Aldo and wondering what on earth was wrong with him. He and I had always understood each other pretty well . . . until tonight.

Night is a funny time. It's the time when most of us hamsters are the most active. And it's the time when most humans are sleepy. It's a good time for thinking, but sometimes thinking can turn to worrying, at least for me.

I wasn't just worried because I couldn't understand Aldo. I was also worried about what would happen if the fire alarm started beeping at night.

Who would carry Og and me outside? At least I knew how to STOP-DROP-ROLL, thanks to that nice firefighter Jeff.

Then I remembered my lock-that-doesn't-lock. While it appeared to be locked to humans, I could open it and come and go as I pleased. So, in case of a fire, I could escape if I had to. That was a relief. But what about Og? Then I remembered that he had popped the top off his tank a few times before. Somehow, I knew that Og and I would scurry, hurry and hop our way to safety.

Once I worked that out, I felt a LOT-LOT-LOT better and the next thing I knew, the morning bell was ringing and another day of school was about to begin.

> SURPRISE: Something totally unexpected and unplanned for. A surprise can be good, like a postcard from Ms Mac. Or a surprise can be bad, like Ms Mac moving to Brazil. A surprise can be good and bad, like a shiny balloon (a good thing) that suddenly pops and scares you (a bad thing).
>
> *Humphrey's Dictionary of Wonderful Words*

3

Hamster on a Roll

I learned a lot about human behaviour during my first seven months in Room 26. I had already worked out a lot about what makes people tick. Humans can be funny, sad, happy and angry . . . all in one day! But the one person I can't quite understand is Mrs Brisbane. Just when I think I understand her, she does something she's never ever done before.

For instance, every single morning she comes into the classroom, puts her books on her desk and her handbag in the desk drawer, checks her hair in the mirror, then walks towards the window and says, 'Good morning, guys. Here's hoping for another great day!'

I always tell her that I'm sure it will be unsqueakably great and Og sometimes answers with his goofy 'BOING!'

But on Tuesday, for the first time all year, she came into the room, dumped her books on the desk, put her handbag in the drawer and slammed it shut. Then she walked over to the noticeboard and stared at the cut-outs of the planets that were up there. 'I wonder how many noticeboards I've put up and taken down over the years?' she asked.

I hoped she wasn't asking me because I didn't have an exact answer. I did know that Mrs Brisbane had been teaching for many years, so the answer would be LOTS-LOTS-LOTS.

She shook her head and began taking down the cut-out picture of planets with interesting names like Neptune, Jupiter and Saturn.

Then there was Mars, which is an angry-looking red colour, with spots on it that look like big scary eyes, especially at night. I wasn't sorry to see that picture go.

The noticeboard was empty by the time the students started streaming in. For months, they'd come in bundled up in coats and boots, hats and gloves. Now they had on light jackets and sweaters and it didn't take long for them to hang their things in the cloakroom and hurry to their seats.

I-Heard-That-Kirk Chen came bounding into the room with a big smile on his face.

'Mrs Brisbane, I'm sorry about yesterday. To

make up for it, I have a surprise for Humphrey. Can I give it to him now?' he asked.

A surprise for *me*? That got my whiskers wiggling.

And it started Gail giggling. 'What is it?' she said. 'Let me see!'

Soon, the other students were gathered around Kirk, begging him to let them see the surprise.

'Okay, Kirk. What is it?' asked Mrs Brisbane. Her arms were folded and she had a suspicious look on her face. After all, Kirk had done a few things that would make any teacher unhappy. Once, he put a cushion on Richie's chair that made a VERY-VERY-VERY rude noise when Richie sat on it. He called it a 'whoopee cushion'. My friends laughed so hard (including Richie), they all wanted a chance to sit on it, but Mrs Brisbane took it away and made Kirk sit in the cloakroom for a while.

This time, Mrs Brisbane held out her hand. 'Let me see it, Kirk,' she said. Dear me, she really didn't trust him.

Kirk reached into his backpack and pulled out something I couldn't see. All of my friends went 'Ooh' and 'Aah,' which made my heart thump faster and faster.

'Can you see it, Og?' I squeaked to my tablemate.

There was no answer.

'It's a hamster ball. We can put Humphrey inside and he can roll around the classroom. See, there are air holes in it. It's good exercise,' Kirk explained. 'Can we try it?'

The thought of rolling around the classroom during the day was so exciting, I climbed up on my ladder to get a closer look.

Mrs Brisbane held the clear yellow ball in her hand. 'Well,' she said, 'I suppose it would be nice for Humphrey. But we have to be careful that we don't step on him or that he doesn't roll some-where dangerous.'

My friends all cheered and I joined in. Og started splashing, so I knew he approved.

'*And* we can't let this interfere with our school work. Testing is coming up, you know,' Mrs Brisbane said with a frown.

Kirk had already opened my cage.

'Don't hurt him,' said Golden Miranda, who's always looking out for me.

Kirk placed me in the ball, then snapped the top shut.

'Make sure it's closed tightly, please,' Speak-Up-Sayeh said softly. She was shy, but she always looked out for me, too.

It was a bit weird being enclosed in a round object. Since it was yellow plastic, the world looked yellow to me and Miranda was more golden than ever. I checked to see that there were holes in the plastic. YES-YES-YES! I wouldn't have trouble breathing.

'Careful now,' warned Mrs Brisbane as Kirk set the ball on the floor at the front of the classroom.

My fellow students crouched down to watch.

'Go on, Humphrey Dumpty,' said A.J. 'Make the ball go.'

Let me tell you, it's very strange to be inside a ball. For one thing, there's nothing flat to stand on, like a floor. So even standing still, the ball felt wobbly.

'Run, Humphrey,' said Seth. 'Get it moving!'

I hesitated for a little bit, but when I heard Og go 'BOING!' I knew I had to move.

I went slowly at first, just moving my paws along at a slow jog. My friends moved back to give me room to roll down the centre aisle.

'Go, Humphrey, go!' said Kirk.

I jogged a little faster.

'Go, Humphrey, go!' the other students chanted. 'Go, go, go!'

I liked the encouragement and I liked the feeling of going fast, so I began to run. It was like spinning my wheel, only this time I was actually going some-where!

Many times before, I'd scurried across the floor of the classroom, but never when the other students were there. As I zoomed down the aisle between the tables and chairs, my friends followed behind me.

The bell rang, which meant school had begun, but once I got rolling, I didn't know how to stop. As much fun as the hamster ball was, it was SCARY-SCARY-SCARY, too, because I couldn't control where I was going.

I heard Mrs Brisbane say, 'Class, we need to begin our work!' But I was on a roll, heading right for – eek! – the wall!

Someone gasped. I think it was Miranda. 'He'll crash!' she said. 'Stop him!'

I tried to slow down but it was too late. The ball bounced off the wall and shot back towards the aisle. I was now upside-down, and before I could get back on my feet, I came to a stop that was so sudden, I did a double flip inside the ball. I looked up and saw a large foot in a sensible black shoe.

It was Mrs Brisbane's foot.

'Class, I want you all in your seats. Take out a sheet of paper for the dictionary exercise. I'll take attendance while you get started.'

I was catching my breath when she leaned down over me. 'And you, young man, will settle down.'

When Mrs Brisbane talks like that, nobody argues with her, especially not a small golden hamster enclosed in a ball. Once she removed her foot, I cautiously headed back down the centre aisle between the desks.

Mrs Brisbane kept a close eye on me while my friends took the test. Usually, I took the test along with them, writing the answers in my notebook. But I was enjoying my freedom a little too much for that. I kept on jogging up and down the centre aisle, but now I was careful to slow to a stop before hitting a wall. That way, I just tapped it, rolled backward, then turned my body inside the ball and jogged towards the opposite wall again.

My friends wrote quietly while Mrs Brisbane gave out the words. I tried not to make too much noise as I sailed past Don't-Complain-Mandy Payne's shiny red shoes, Pay-Attention-Art's black basketball boots and Garth's scuffed white trainers. Sit-Still-Seth's feet TAP-TAP-TAPPED as he wrote.

I don't know how many times I went back and forth but it was getting a little boring. If only I could turn the thing! After the test papers were collected, Mrs Brisbane said it was time to finish the Spring into Numbers project. I think my friends forgot about me while they cut and pasted, coloured and stapled their papers.

By break time, Room 26 looked completely different. The noticeboard was covered with cut-outs of flowers, rabbits and robins – but they all had maths problems on them. Plus and minus numbers, multiplying and dividing numbers peeked out from the leaves of the blossoms and ran up and down the rabbit ears and robin wings.

Tabitha and Richie made clouds in all kinds of shapes – even triangles and squares. Gail and Sayeh tacked a row of colourful flowers all around the blackboard. There was a pattern to the colours and it took me a while to work it out. Garth and A.J. made a huge kite with a LONG-LONG-LONG tail that had a LONG-LONG-LONG problem on it.

I began to jog with joy. Spring was bright! Spring was happy! Spring was fun!

While Mrs Brisbane helped hang the kite, I suddenly hit the leg of Seth's desk and veered off towards the door, which was open to let in the spring breeze.

I sailed out of Room 26 and not one of my friends noticed.

'HELP-HELP-HELP!' I squeaked. In the distance, I heard Og's 'BOING!' but everything was completely silent in the corridor. As I rolled out of Room 26, towards the side door, I wondered if I'd end up on the playground again. I frantically tried to guide the ball away from the door, but it wouldn't turn quickly enough.

Luckily, the door was closed tightly so I bounced off it. I was heading towards another door. It was FAR-FAR-FAR away, past a long row of classroom doors. Suddenly, I wished Aldo hadn't polished the floor quite so well. I also wished the hamster ball had brakes. The best I could do to slow it down was to stop moving my legs.

What an unsqueakably dangerous situation for a small hamster! At least my cage had that lock-that-doesn't-lock. But there was no way for me to get out of the ball.

'Goodbye, Room 26!' I squeaked.

Suddenly I heard a piercingly loud noise. (Hamsters are very sensitive creatures and we don't appreciate loud noises.)

'Stop right there,' a voice firmly ordered me. The ball stopped abruptly and this time I did a triple flip. But I recognized the voice . . . and the shrill sound. It was Mrs Wright and her whistle. She was standing right in front of me with one of her huge white puffy shoes resting on top of the ball.

Just for fun, I suppose, she blew her whistle again.

'Mrs Brisbane!' she bellowed.

Mrs Brisbane rushed out into the corridor and hurried towards us. 'What's wrong, Mrs Wright?'

That sounded funny, but I wasn't in the mood to laugh. I was afraid Mrs Wright might blow her whistle again.

'I just happened to be coming down the corridor when I found your *rat* out here!'

'For goodness' sake!' Mrs Brisbane leaned down

and picked up the ball. 'How did you get out here?'

'You created a very dangerous situation,' said Mrs Wright. 'Someone could trip over him and get hurt.'

'Well, no one did,' said Mrs Brisbane. 'Don't worry, it won't happen again.'

Mrs Wright sniffed loudly. 'Still, I must report this to Mr Morales.'

'Do whatever you think you should.' Mrs Brisbane sounded a little snippy and I was GLAD-GLAD-GLAD. 'Come on, Humphrey.'

My classmates gathered at the door, waiting for my return.

'Back in your seats,' Mrs Brisbane told them. 'And you, Humphrey, are going back in your cage.'

I was so happy to be back in my cage, I took a long drink of water, then headed straight for my sleeping hut and a nice long doze.

WHISTLE: A shiny device which, when someone blows it, makes an ear-splitting sound that can seriously hurt the delicate ears of small creatures like hamsters. *Use whistles sparingly, if at all.* (Some humans can whistle without a device, but hamsters never can.)
Humphrey's Dictionary of Wonderful Words

4

Spring Fever

'Wait-For-The-Bell-Garth.'

Mrs Brisbane's words jolted me from my nap.

Garth always jumped out of his chair just before the bell rang for break, lunch or the end of the day. When Mrs Brisbane reminded him, he sat back down again until the bell actually rang.

'Now you may go, class,' Mrs Brisbane said.

Once the room was empty, she shuffled the papers on her desk. Then the door opened and in came Mr Morales.

'Got a second, Sue?' he asked.

'Of course,' Mrs Brisbane greeted him. 'What can I do for you?'

'Ruth Wright put in a complaint. It's about . . .'

Mrs Brisbane finished his sentence. '. . . Humphrey.'

The head smiled. 'Yeah. Just try and keep him in the classroom.'

'I intend to,' said Mrs Brisbane.

'Don't worry,' Mr Morales chuckled. 'She also complained about the squeaky door in the cafeteria, some fingerprints on the trophy case and the fact that the clocks are running thirty seconds slow.'

'Well, she teaches PE. I guess rules are very important to her.'

Mr Morales strolled over to my cage. 'So Humphrey had a little adventure today? Maybe he has spring fever,' he said.

'I think the whole class does,' Mrs Brisbane answered. 'It happens every year. The weather turns nice and the class gets silly.'

The head leaned in close to my cage. 'Well, no more silliness from you, Humphrey. You stay put.'

'I will try because that Mrs Wright is MEAN-MEAN-MEAN!' I squeaked.

Mr Morales chuckled. 'Oh, don't let it bother you, Humphrey. Mrs Wright likes to complain.'

Then he turned back to Mrs Brisbane. 'Don't forget, deadline's coming up, Sue.'

'Sorry, I forgot. I'll write myself a note.'

Mr Morales smiled. 'Great.'

The bell rang again and the head excused himself. In seconds, my classmates came racing back into the room, pink-cheeked, out of breath and smiling. At least most of them were smiling.

'Good game, Tabby,' Seth told Tabitha. 'We almost won.'

'Yeah, we would have if it wasn't for you-know-who,' she answered.

Then she glanced at Garth, who was right behind her. He definitely wasn't smiling.

'Take your seats, children,' said Mrs Brisbane. 'Get out your social studies books and turn to page 112.'

Sometimes being a classroom hamster is like being a detective. You hear little bits of conversation and try to work out what's going on. Like, what was that about Mrs Brisbane forgetting something Mr Morales wanted? She never forgets anything! And why did Tabitha say 'you-know-who' instead of Garth's name? And why wasn't Garth happy, like everybody else?

I was sorting out my thoughts when something even more puzzling happened.

Instead of reading his social studies book, Garth was writing something in big letters on a piece of paper but I couldn't see what he wrote.

He kept the paper on his desk and read the book, but he stopped to look at the paper once in a while. Then he wrote another word next to it.

I climbed up my ladder to see if I could get a better look at it.

'Og?' I squeaked softly. 'Can you see what Garth wrote on that paper?'

I heard some gentle splashing but no answer.

Mrs Brisbane started writing questions on the board, and soon my friends were busily writing the answers. This went on until the lunch bell rang.

My classmates all got up and headed for the door. Garth pushed forward, clutching the paper in his hand. He paused near A.J.'s desk and dropped the paper in front of his friend, then hurried towards the door. A.J. stared at the piece of paper, crumbled it into a ball and dropped it on the floor. (Oh dear, Aldo wouldn't like that!)

When Mrs Brisbane got ready to leave for lunch, she spotted the paper on the floor, picked it up and smoothed it out. She frowned when she read it, then put it on *her* desk and left the room.

'Something is unsqueakably wrong between Garth and A.J.,' I told Og. 'I've got to know what that paper says!'

It's a LONG-LONG-LONG way from the table where Og and I live to Mrs Brisbane's desk and it's a perilous journey, but once I'm curious about something, I can't get it out of my furry hamster head.

'Keep a look-out, Oggy, okay?' I told my friend. 'I'm going over there.'

He answered with a reassuring 'BOING!'

I pushed on the lock-that-doesn't-lock and the door swung open. I took a deep breath, and as I had done before, grabbed onto the leg of the table and slid down so fast, I could feel the breeze ruffling my fur.

I zigzagged across the room, happy to be outside the ball, since I didn't have to worry about bouncing off tables or chairs. I quickly reached Mrs Brisbane's desk at the opposite side of the room. I can't tell you how unsqueakably tall it looks from a hamster's point of view.

Between the chair legs were two horizontal wooden bars. I reached UP-UP-UP, grabbed the lowest bar and slowly pulled myself up.

'Are you watching the clock, Og?' I squeaked.

'BOING!' Og answered.

Grabbing the next bar, I used all my strength to pull myself up. I was getting tired, but knowing that lunch didn't last very long, I wrapped my legs around the chair leg and slowly inched my way up to the seat of the chair.

I sat on the chair seat for a few seconds, trying to catch my breath. I was still a long way from the desktop and that piece of paper. Above my head, there was a desk drawer with a handle on it. I had to leap up to grab hold of it – oooh, cold and slippery – and then I reached up for the edge of the desk and pulled myself up again, finally flinging my whole body onto the surface of the desk.

I lay there on my stomach, muscles quivering from all that work. It's a good thing I work out every day on my wheel and my ladder. It helps strengthen my arms. Or my legs. Or whatever.

'BOING-BOING!' said Og and I didn't need to look at the clock to know I needed to hurry things along. I sat up and saw the piece of paper laid out neatly before me. Of course, to my small eyes the letters were huge – I had to squint and strain to finally make out what it said:

DIRTY RAT

That was it? I'd come all this way and put myself in great danger to read the words 'dirty rat'? I had no idea what Garth was getting at, although I knew that being called a rat, which sometimes happens to me, is not supposed to be a compliment.

Og began splashing wildly. I glanced up at the clock and OH-OH-OH, I barely had time to get back!

I had to take the quickest (though not the safest) route back, so I slid down the side of the desk, landed on the floor with a large thump, raced across the room and grabbed onto the cord of the blinds, which I always used for swinging myself back up to the table.

'BOING-BOING-BOING-BOING!' Og sounded like the fire alarm, but all I could think about was getting back to my cage on time. I heard the bell ring as I skittered across the table and swung the cage door shut behind me.

Every muscle in my small body ached.

'BOING!' Og twanged.

'The paper . . . says . . . "dirty rat",' I told him, panting from all my effort. 'But don't . . . ask me why.'

All that work and I still didn't know what was going on!

My classmates began to trickle in from lunch. As usual, Miranda was with her best friend Sayeh, and other best friends were together: Heidi and Gail, Seth and Tabitha, A.J. and – whoa! It was very unusual to see A.J. without Garth.

A.J. slid into his seat first. When Garth sat down, A.J. leaned over. I strained my small furry ears to hear. 'What was that about? That "dirty rat" thing?'

Garth glared at A.J. 'Friends don't pick their best friends last. Rats do.'

'You're my friend,' A.J. protested. 'You're just not very good at sport.'

'Like I need you to remind me,' muttered Garth.

Right then, Mrs Brisbane started to talk about seeds sprouting, and there was no chance to learn more about the trouble between Garth and A.J.

'Wait-After-Class-Garth,' Mrs Brisbane said when the bell rang at the end of the day.

'Og, did you hear that?' I asked. 'She didn't say Wait-For-The-Bell-Garth. She said Wait-After-Class-Garth.'

Og splashed a bit, but I'm pretty sure he heard, too.

The room emptied quickly and soon Garth was alone with Mrs Brisbane.

Being kept in after class is never a good thing, at least in my experience. And in my months in Room 26, a number of my friends had been kept after school.

Mrs Brisbane went to her desk and picked up the crumpled paper. 'Did you write this, Garth?'

Garth shrugged his shoulders.

'It looks like your writing,' the teacher continued.

'I was just messing around,' answered Garth.

'I found it under A.J.'s desk,' Mrs Brisbane explained. 'I thought the two of you were friends.'

'We're not friends.' Garth wrinkled his nose. 'Not any more.'

Mrs Brisbane sat down and looked thoughtful. 'Would you tell me what happened?'

'I've got to catch my bus,' Garth answered, looking towards the door.

'Think about it and we'll talk tomorrow.' Mrs Brisbane folded up the piece of paper and dropped it in her handbag. 'I'll just hold onto this.'

Garth raced out of the door without looking back. Mrs Brisbane stayed sitting in the chair. She stared at the student tables, the noticeboard, the blackboard. She looked at the room as if she'd never seen it before.

After a while, she picked up her books and her handbag and came over to adjust the blinds. 'I hope you two can get along for the rest of the night,' she told Og and me.

'We'll TRY-TRY-TRY!' I assured her, and I meant it.

Og didn't say anything, but I don't think he was annoyed at me or anything like that.

Maybe he just had spring fever.

RAT: A perfectly nice rodent with a bad reputation. Some rats even make nice pets. There are rats of all shapes and sizes, but when one human calls another human a rat, it's never meant as a compliment.

Humphrey's Dictionary of Wonderful Words

5

Surprise from Outer Space

I don't know if I had spring fever, but I did have aching muscles following my adventure that afternoon. Besides that, I had a funny feeling in my tummy after I read the note that said 'dirty rat'.

I ate a good helping of Nutri-Nibbles, but my stomach still felt weird.

Later, Og and I were both in a somewhat dreamy state when the door opened, the lights came on and I heard a familiar squeaking sound.

'It's Aldo!' I rushed to the front of my cage to greet my friend. I was hoping he would be a little easier to understand than he had been the night before.

'BOING!' Og sounded quite alarmed and I could see why.

There was Aldo's trolley, piled high with his broom, his mop and pail, lots of spray bottles and cloths and rubbish bags to be filled.

And there was someone pushing the trolley, just as Aldo did every night during the week.

But that person was NOT-NOT-NOT Aldo!

'Eeek!' I squeaked.

The person with the trolley was much shorter than Aldo. The person had no moustache and had longer hair, pulled back in a ponytail. The person had on a red sweatshirt and grey trousers and black trainers.

That person was definitely a girl. Or a woman. A female, anyway. And there was something strange about the way she moved. She tugged at her ear, snapped her fingers and swung her arms in an odd rhythm. Still, she straightened the desks, swept the floor, then mopped it (which Aldo didn't do every night). She even dusted the shelf where Og and I live, but she didn't seem to notice we were there.

'How do you do?' I squeaked up as politely as possible. 'Could you please tell me, WHAT DID YOU DO WITH ALDO?'

Og seemed quite upset as he hopped up and down, up and down, repeating one 'BOING' after another.

The person who was cleaning didn't even seem to notice. As she swept closer to my cage, I saw there was a device attached to her ear!

'Og,' I said nervously, 'I saw a film at Seth's house once about an alien from another planet, and that alien acted very strangely. A bit like this person.'

Og stopped hopping and started listening.

'You don't think she could be one of *them*?' I asked. 'Because in that movie, the space aliens captured a human and took him to their planet. I mean, you don't think that happened to Aldo, do you?'

Og stayed very quiet. In the film, the space alien had wires in his head, too.

I was sorry I'd seen that movie, because it made me think scary thoughts.

'See that thing in her ear? She could be getting signals from the mother ship.' I tried not to become hysterical. 'That's what they called it in the film – the mother ship.'

Finally, the person, who had done a very nice cleaning job for a creature from outer space, wheeled the trolley out of the door. She turned off the lights (without opening the blinds the way Aldo always did) and left Room 26.

The room was quiet, except for the TICK-TICK-TICK of the clock, which seemed to be louder than usual.

Suddenly, the lights came back on. The person walked back in without the cleaning trolley. She came over to my cage and reached into her pocket.

'A ray gun, Og! The space aliens in the movie had ray guns so they could capture the Earthlings!' I squeaked.

She pulled out a small carrot and shoved it between the bars of my cage. Then she left again, turning out the lights so we were plunged into darkness.

'Eeek!' I squeaked. When my eyes adjusted to the dark, I stared at the little carrot. 'I don't suppose that's really a ray gun,' I said. 'But it could be an alien carrot.'

'BOING!' Og agreed.

It was nice of the creature to give me a carrot, but I have to admit I didn't touch it. Not all night long. You can't be too sure about aliens, you know.

And I still had no idea what had happened to my good friend Aldo.

˙ö˙

The world looked normal again in the light of day, and the morning went along like any morning in Room 26, except for the fact that Garth and A.J. were both very quiet. In fact, they never even looked at each other.

Then came time for break.

While Mrs Brisbane wrote word problems on the board, I spun on my wheel, knowing my friends were out exercising on the playground.

Suddenly, the door swung open and in walked Mrs Wright, pulling Garth along with her. He looked very unhappy.

'Mrs Brisbane, you'll have to do something about this boy!' the PE teacher announced.

Mrs Brisbane was truly surprised. 'Garth? What happened?'

'You know our students are required to get a certain amount of physical activity at break every day,' said Mrs Wright. 'But I found this young man hiding behind the building when he was supposed to be playing ball. *Strictly* against the rules.'

'Were you hiding, Garth?' Mrs Brisbane asked.

'Sort of,' he mumbled.

Mrs Brisbane told Mrs Wright that she'd take care of the situation.

'What will you do?' the PE teacher asked, fingering her whistle.

'That's between Garth and me.' There was ice in Mrs Brisbane's voice. 'Thank you, Mrs Wright.'

Mrs Wright left, thank goodness, and Mrs Brisbane asked Garth to sit down. She sat down next to him.

'Why weren't you playing ball with your friends?' she asked.

'Don't have any,' said Garth. His face was squinched up like he was going to cry.

'Of course you do, Garth,' Mrs Brisbane insisted. 'You have lots of friends.'

Garth shook his head. 'Not any more.'

Mrs Brisbane spoke very softly. 'Please tell me what happened.'

'I'm lousy at softball and when they choose teams, I always get picked last.' Garth's voice quavered. 'Yesterday, A.J. was the team captain and got to pick his players and he picked me last, even though I'm his best friend. I mean, I *was* his best friend. He even picked Sayeh before me and she's not very good either. Then Tabitha told Seth they lost because of me. So I decided not to play any more.'

He sniffled and Mrs Brisbane handed him a tissue.

'I'm sure that hurt a lot. It always hurt me when I got picked last. I wasn't very good at sport,' she confided.

'But you're a *girl*,' Garth told her. 'Girls don't have to be good.'

Mrs Brisbane smiled a little. 'I understand that Tabitha is the best player in the class and she's a girl.'

'Yeah, but still, it's different being a boy.' Garth sighed. 'A.J. would probably pick Humphrey ahead of me.'

Well, yes, he might. I'm very popular with my friends. I don't how you play softball, but I have to admit, I was good at hamster ball.

Garth and Mrs Brisbane sat in silence for a while until I just couldn't stand it any longer.

'I think A.J. was MEAN-MEAN-MEAN not to pick Garth,' I blurted out.

'It sounds like Humphrey has something to say on the subject,' said the teacher.

Garth didn't even smile.

'Tell you what,' she continued. 'You and A.J. bring your lunches in here today and we'll talk.'

'He'll think I told on him!' Garth protested.

'I'll make sure he doesn't,' Mrs Brisbane assured him. 'But I can't make him choose you first.'

'Even if he'd picked me third or fourth, it would have been okay,' said Garth. 'Just not *last*.'

Mrs Brisbane glanced at the clock and said that break was almost over. She asked him to feed Og some of his yucky crickets, something Garth likes to do.

I headed for my sleeping hut to think about what I'd just heard. I didn't know a thing about softball. I'd never been chosen for a team, either. But I knew one thing: I wouldn't want to be picked last, especially by my best friend.

⋅ȯ⋅

Lunchtime rolled around and Mrs Brisbane told Garth and A.J. to bring their lunches to the classroom. This was a surprising thing that had never happened before, like being in a hamster ball or having Aldo captured by aliens.

A.J. brought his lunch from home in a bright-blue bag. Garth carried his in on a tray and it smelled yummy. Mrs Brisbane took a container of yoghurt and a spoon out of her bag.

But no one, not even Mrs Brisbane, ate a bite.

'A.J., Mrs Wright said that you picked a very good softball team yesterday,' she began.

'Yes, ma'am,' said A.J. loudly.

'But she was surprised that you didn't pick Garth until last.'

A.J. stared down at the untouched sandwich in front of him.

'I was surprised, too,' the teacher continued. 'Since you're such good friends.'

'Yes, ma'am,' said A.J. 'It's just that Garth's not the best player. And I think when you're choosing a team, you've got to pick the best players. Don't you?'

'I suppose so,' said Mrs Brisbane. 'How do you feel about that, Garth?'

Garth squirmed in his chair. 'It wouldn't have hurt him to pick me. I ended up on the team any-way.'

'So it made you feel bad to be picked last?' Mrs Brisbane asked.

'Yes.' Garth looked miserable. So did A.J.

'Somebody's got to be picked last,' said A.J. 'The rest of the team would have been annoyed if I picked you before somebody like Richie or Kirk.'

'I never thought of that,' said Mrs Brisbane, stirring the yoghurt with her spoon.

'Well, now *I'm* annoyed, because it feels really awful to be picked last,' said Garth. His cheeks were flaming red.

'I should think it does,' Mrs Brisbane agreed.

As far as I could see, the conversation was going nowhere. Back and forth, back and forth. Mrs Brisbane agreed with both of them, but neither boy changed his mind. Not one bit.

'I imagine A.J. is sorry you felt bad,' said Mrs Brisbane. 'Right?'

'Well . . . yeah.' A.J. didn't sound totally convinced but at least he agreed.

'And I'll bet Garth realizes what a hard decision it was for you, A.J.,' she added. 'Right, Garth?'

'Yeah . . .'

Garth sounded like he had more to say, but Mrs Brisbane didn't let him. 'Good. Then you two can play ball together and be friends as well. After all, softball is only a game. It shouldn't be important enough to break up a friendship. Agreed?'

The boys nodded. They didn't have much choice.

Mrs Brisbane wasn't quite finished. 'Then at the next break, you'll play ball, won't you, Garth?'

Garth groaned. 'I'll just strike out and then everybody will be annoyed at me.'

'You don't keep your eye on the ball,' A.J. blurted out.

'I do too,' Garth snapped back. 'I keep my eye on it as it sails past my bat.'

Mrs Brisbane glanced at the clock. 'Eat your lunches now. You've got to keep your strength up for the next game.'

She sounded very cheery, but Garth and A.J. looked about as un-cheery as two people could be. They ate their lunches in silence until I couldn't stand it any more.

'For goodness' sake, make up!' I squeaked.

Mrs Brisbane craned her neck to look at me. 'I didn't know you were so interested in sport, Humphrey,' she said. The boys finally smiled a little.

I don't know much about sport but I do know about Garth and A.J. And if Mrs Brisbane couldn't get them to be friends again, I suppose I'd have to.

It's just that I didn't have a single idea about how I'd do it.

ALIEN: Somebody – or something – from another land or even another planet. Aliens can be any shape, size, colour . . . but they usually want to take you to their leader.

Humphrey's Dictionary of Wonderful Words

The Space Alien Squeaks

Later that afternoon, when it was time for break again, Mrs Brisbane asked Garth to stay inside.

He looked pretty miserable because I guess he thought he was in trouble again. But once the other students had left, Mrs Brisbane told Garth he could read or erase the blackboard for her or work on his homework.

'You're not in trouble, Garth,' she explained. 'I just thought you'd like a change from break, just for today.'

He clearly did, because that was the cleanest blackboard I've ever seen.

Once school was out, I didn't have much time to worry about Garth and A.J. I had creatures from outer space on my mind.

'Og, I've been thinking about that alien movie I saw at Seth's house,' I told my neighbour. 'They talked a funny language. Like they said "*roka mata*" instead of "hello". And "*oobo trill*" instead of "goodbye". They could understand each other but no humans could understand them.'

'BOING!' Og sounded truly alarmed.

'I was thinking – that night Aldo talked so strangely, maybe he'd already been taken over by space aliens.'

'BOING-BOING!' Og replied.

'But the alien – or whoever she was – didn't say a word last night. Maybe she will, if she comes back tonight.'

I was feeling shivery and quivery just thinking that a creature from another planet might return to Room 26.

The clock loudly ticked off the minutes as the room grew darker.

'It won't be long now, Oggy,' I squeaked.

Og splashed around in the water. How I wish he could really talk so I could understand him!

Then I heard it: the SQUEAK-SQUEAK-SQUEAKING of the cleaning trolley. My heart skipped a beat. Maybe Aldo would be back! I'd be so happy to see him, I wouldn't care what came out of his mouth.

The lights came on and the trolley rolled into the

room. It took my eyes a few seconds to get used to the bright light. When I did, I saw who was pushing the trolley. It was the creature from the night before, only this time she had a hood over her head. I couldn't see if the device was attached to her ear or not.

As she went about her work, I wondered why space aliens would come to earth to clean Room 26. And I wondered what this creature had done to Aldo. Just thinking about my missing friend made me angry. What was her evil plan? Suddenly, I wasn't scared any more.

'PLEASE-PLEASE-PLEASE tell us what you did with Aldo!' I demanded.

Either the aliens on the mother ship told her to ignore me or she didn't hear me. She just kept on sweeping.

Suddenly, there was a loud sound – not exactly music but not exactly a ringing either. It sounded like the music of another planet.

The mother ship was calling!

The alien cleaner reached up and touched her ear. The music stopped.

'Hi. Yeah, it's me. I'm cleaning.'

WHAT-WHAT-WHAT was going on? First she has Aldo saying things I don't understand, and now *she* speaks English.

'I'm finished with the programme. Yeah, I don't

take off for Spurling till summer.' She hesitated, then laughed. 'Don't worry. It'll be a while before I'm performing surgery on people. Listen, I'll ring you later. Bye.'

She touched her ear again. Then she pulled a tiny piece of cauliflower out of her pocket. She walked to my cage and dropped the cauliflower between the bars.

'Here,' she said.

Without another word, she pushed the trolley through the door, turned out the lights and was gone.

It took me a few seconds before I could squeak at all. 'Og?' I said. 'Did you see that? She can talk to the mother ship through her ear. And she's taking off for Spurling. Ever hear of that planet?'

'BOING!' he answered, but it wasn't much help.

Spurling had not been one of the planets on our noticeboard, but I remembered that Mrs Brisbane had said there were other solar systems. Maybe this strange creature was from one that was FAR-FAR-FAR away.

But that wasn't what made me feel shivery and quivery. 'Did you hear her say she'll be performing surgery on *people*?'

'BOING-BOING-BOING-BOING!' Og was clearly alarmed. So was I.

'Maybe that's why she captured Aldo,' I said. My

heart was pounding. 'Some kind of experiment. Thank goodness she said it won't be for a while.'

Og's response was a huge splash as he dived into his tank.

I stared at the piece of cauliflower. It's usually one of my favourite crunchy vegetables, but just to be on the safe side I hid it down in the corner of my bedding, with the alien carrot.

I was relieved to see that they didn't glow in the dark.

It was unusually dark in the room that night, since the creature didn't open the blinds the way Aldo always did. Surprisingly, I dozed off. But I didn't have a very restful night because of my dream.

I'm sure most humans would be surprised to learn that I dream when I sleep. Humans seem surprised at everything I do. 'Look, he's spinning that wheel,' they'll say. Or 'Ooh, he's washing his face!' (That isn't even accurate as I don't exactly use soap and water.)

They'd be even more surprised at the things they *don't* see me doing, like escaping from my cage and helping my friends solve their problems. Or writing in my notebook, which is something most hamsters don't do.

But they'd be *flabbergasted* (now that's a word for my dictionary) by my dreams.

Especially the one I had that night.

There I was, standing next to a space ship that looked a lot like Aldo's cleaning trolley. It was parked in front of Longfellow School and I was surrounded by creatures that looked exactly like green, glowing carrots!

'Take us to your leader,' one of them commanded me.

I was very confused because I couldn't decide whether to take them to Mrs Brisbane, who is certainly my leader in Room 26, or Mr Morales, who is the leader of the whole of Longfellow School.

The alien carrots moved in closer.

'Take us to your leader,' they began to chant. 'Leader, leader, leader!'

'*Oobo trill*,' I said, remembering that those words meant 'goodbye' in the movie I'd seen.

Then I took off running across the car park with the alien carrot-people following close on my heels.

'Og, help me!' I called out. 'Oggy!'

Suddenly, I saw my green goggle-eyed friend gliding towards me, riding the top of his tank (the TOP-THAT-POPS) like a skateboard.

'SCREEE!' he shouted.

I hopped onto the back of the speeding top and we zipped across the car park, leaving the space beings far behind.

When I woke up, I sleepily squeaked, 'Thanks, Og,' before I dozed off again – and this time I didn't dream at all.

•ö•

The next day, I was busy worrying about how it feels to be picked last for a team, and about space aliens whisking Aldo off to the mother ship (wherever that was).

Somehow, I had to let people know what had happened to Aldo. His wife Maria would be worried, as well as his nephew Richie Rinaldi, who was a student in Room 26. I watched Richie carefully in class, but he seemed just the same as ever. Maybe he didn't know his uncle was missing yet. Still, on Thursday morning, I woke up with a Plan.

It's very important to have a Plan when you want to accomplish something important, like saving a friend from beings from outer space.

I got my idea while watching my classmates finish off the noticeboard. Mrs Brisbane brought out a big pile of shiny cut-out letters. She used them to spell out S-P-R-I-N-G. There were a lot of extra letters left over, neatly stacked on the floor right under the noticeboard.

When Mrs Brisbane and the students left for lunch, I made my move.

'Og, I have an idea, but I don't have time to

explain it. Will you watch the clock for me?'

'BOING-BOING!' Og twanged.

If there was one thing that frog was good for, it was for keeping watch when I was out of my cage. More than once he had warned me when I was running out of time.

I flung open the cage door (thank goodness for that lock-that-doesn't-lock), glided across the table and slid down the leg.

Once I was on the floor, I had a clear shot between the desks and wasted no time in getting to the letters.

But once I was up close, I realized that they were MUCH-MUCH-MUCH bigger than I had expected. Probably five times bigger than I am, maybe more.

Still, when I have a Plan, I don't let anything stand in my way.

'Watch the time, Oggy!' I called out.

Og assured me with a giant 'BOING!'

I stared up at the tall stack of letters. This was going to be a test of strength . . . and a test of my spelling!

When I first had the idea, I'd thought of spelling out something like this:

HELP! ALDO HAS BEEN CAPTURED BY SPACE ALIENS!

But with such big letters and so little time, I quickly changed my plan of attack. First, I had to get the letters on the ground, so I backed away, then ran forward at top speed.

'Hee-yah!' I closed my eyes as I hit the stack of letters, sending them scattering in all directions.

'BOING!' warned Og.

I glanced up at the big clock. Og was right. I didn't have a lot of time left, so I quickly went to work. Let me tell you, it's not easy to read those tall letters when you're a small hamster and they're lying flat on the ground. I stood on my tippy toes so I could get a better look.

Luckily, there were several As to choose from. I picked a red one and pulled it out onto the floor. The L was a little more difficult. It was upside-down, which means it looked like a 7. I turned it around and dragged it to the spot next to the A. The I and E were easy.

'BOING-BOING!' Og twanged loudly.

Oh dear. A glance at the clock told me time was passing a little faster than I expected. I turned back and searched for the next letter.

There were plenty of Zs but no Ns in sight. I'm afraid it took me a while to realize that a Z turned on its side looks like an N. And vice versa.

A-L-I-E-N. Not quite right yet, I decided.

'BOING-BOING-BOING!' Og warned.

'Okay, Og. I'm almost finished!' I assured him.

One more letter to go. I didn't want a B. A-L-I-E-N-B would be confusing. I didn't want a C or a V or a W.

'BOING-BOING-BOING-BOING-BOING!'

I didn't dare look at the clock.

'Where are you?' I asked. Just then I saw it.

'Good old S,' I said, pulling the letter into place. A-L-I-E-N-S.

It wasn't a full explanation but it was the best I could do.

'I'm coming back, Og!' I alerted my friend.

I raced across the floor, leaped up to grab the cord of the blinds and madly started it swinging.

'SCREEEEE!' That was Og's most serious warning. As soon as I was almost level with the table, I let go of the cord and slid across the table, landing with a thud right at the door to my cage.

The door to Room 26 opened and I heard the familiar sounds of my friends chatting away as they came into the classroom.

'Take your seats,' Mrs Brisbane told them.

I was at great risk of being discovered as I darted into my cage and pulled the door behind me. Luckily, no one was watching.

'Thanks, Oggy,' I told my neighbour.

All I heard was splashing.

'What on earth . . . ?'

Mrs Brisbane stared down at the letters on the floor. 'Kirk, is this more of your work?'

'Huh?' It wasn't one of Kirk's funniest lines.

'Never mind,' said Mrs Brisbane. 'But remember, April Fools' Day is over now.'

'I didn't do it,' Kirk protested.

'LOOK-LOOK-LOOK!' I squeaked. No one noticed. I glanced at Richie. If only he understood his uncle was in danger. 'Richie, look!'

Richie paid no attention. He was busy scribbling in his notebook.

Mrs Brisbane gathered the letters, stacked them up again and put them on her desk.

All that work for nothing! I was out of breath, out of luck and, for once, out of ideas. So I did the only thing a small hamster can do: I took a nap. After all, I'd need to be alert if aliens from outer space invaded Room 26.

At the end of the day, Mrs Brisbane asked, 'Now, who will be taking Humphrey home this weekend?'

'Me!' a voice called out.

It was Heidi Hopper, of course.

Mrs Brisbane shook her head. 'You didn't raise your hand, Heidi. I think maybe you need another week to work on that. Now, who else would like Humphrey?'

Several hands waved in the air. Over the months,

I'd gone home at least once with all my fellow students and they had all invited me back again.

'Garth, is it all right with your parents?' she asked.

'Yes, ma'am. They signed the paper.' He pulled a crumpled piece of paper out of his pocket and held it up. Mrs Brisbane walked to his desk and looked at it.

'All right, then. Humphrey is going to the Tugwells' house tomorrow,' she announced.

I felt sorry for Heidi, who looked so disappointed.

Garth, on the other hand, looked happy for the first time all week.

DREAM: Like a surprise, a dream can be good or bad. Dreams are pictures you see in your head while you are asleep. Day-dreams, which unlike other dreams happen when you're awake, can be very nice, but teachers don't like them.

Humphrey's Dictionary of
Wonderful Words

7

Surprise Attack

That night, after dark, the being from outer space returned to clean Room 26. As nervous as I was about Aldo's disappearance, I was glad that she'd said she couldn't operate on anyone for a while. She wasn't going to take off for the planet Spurling until summer, so I had a little time to save my friend.

Still, when she came up to my cage with a piece of broccoli, I just had to squeak up. 'Release Aldo right away! And go back to where you came from.'

'Gosh, you're a feisty little thing,' she said.

That was a first. She was talking to *me*. 'You're so cute, I'd like to take you home with me.'

'BOING!' That was Og's reaction.

My reaction was to quiver and shiver, just thinking of being taken to the far-off planet of Spurling, home of the alien carrots.

'BOING-BOING-BOING!' Og twanged.

The creature giggled and then pushed the trolley out of the room and turned out the lights.

The room was dead silent for a few seconds. Maybe longer. At last, I stopped twitching long enough to squeak. 'Og, she wants to capture us!'

Og splashed briskly.

'We can't let her do it!'

He splashed a whole lot more.

I was relieved to be going home with Garth for the weekend. But my friend Og usually stayed in Room 26 for the weekend, since he could go longer without eating than I could. I wouldn't rest easily, knowing Og might be going to outer space while I was having a grand old time with Garth.

'Morning, Sue. Got something for me?' Mr Morales was all smiles when he came into Room 26 on Friday morning. His tie had little kites with red tails trailing down.

'Oh, sorry. I forgot again,' Mrs Brisbane replied.

The head's smile quickly faded. 'Is there a problem, Sue?'

'No, I just forgot. I'll bring it on Monday,' Mrs Brisbane declared.

Mr Morales looked a little worried and I didn't blame him. Mrs Brisbane had NEVER-NEVER-NEVER forgotten anything before. Goodness, if she could forget something important that Mr Morales wanted, she could forget something *else* important, like helping my friends and me learn our vocabulary words!

I was worried about my teacher, and there was more to worry about. Garth and A.J. still weren't acting like old friends. In fact, Garth went to great lengths to avoid A.J., which wasn't easy because their desks were very close.

At the end of the day, A.J. tapped Garth on the shoulder. 'You taking Humphrey on the bus?' he asked.

'No, my mum's picking us up,' Garth replied.

'Can I have a lift?' A.J. was at least trying to be friendly.

'No way. We have to stop somewhere on the way home.' Garth turned his back on A.J. and came over to my cage. I could tell his feelings were still hurt.

He gathered up my cage, food and even the new hamster ball. While he did, I had a last-minute message for Og.

'I wish you were going with me, Og! I hope you'll still be here when I get back!' I squeaked.

'BOING-BOING!' he twanged at the top of his voice.

I wondered if there were any frogs – or hamsters – on the planet Spurling.

'Farewell, froggy friend!' were my parting words.

I'd had several adventures on the bus with A.J. and Garth, but on that day, Garth's mother picked us up in a very tall car. Garth's brother Andy was in the back seat.

'Ham!' Andy shouted. I didn't mind. He was little and didn't know the difference between a hamster and a ham yet.

The ride home was smooth, nothing like the bumpy bus. Strangely enough, we didn't make a stop, like Garth told A.J. Instead, we went straight home.

Once I was settled on the living-room table, I heard an odd twanging noise that reminded me a lot of Og. Could my friend have come along after all?

'BOING!' went the sound. Then 'BLING-BLING.' That didn't sound like Og at all.

Garth came into the room carrying a large stringed instrument. He ran his fingers over the strings and out came the sounds. 'BLING-BLANG-BLING!'

It sounded quite nice.

'How do you like my guitar?' Garth asked.

'It's unsqueakably wonderful!' I replied. I was just sorry all that came out was SQUEAK-SQUEAK-SQUEAK!

'I've been taking lessons,' Garth told me. 'Want to hear a song?'

'Of course.'

He strummed those strings and played a great version of 'Twinkle Twinkle Little Star'. I only heard two mistakes, and they were small ones.

'Bravo!' I squeaked when he was finished.

'Did you like it?' asked Garth. 'Here's one called "Down in the Valley".'

He played it from start to finish, without any mistakes at all that I could hear.

'Bravo!' I shouted again.

My classmates constantly surprise me with their talents. Tabitha and Seth know so much about sport, Sayeh sings beautifully and Art can draw. And ever since his birthday party, where a magician performed, Richie's been doing magic tricks. I could never work out how he did them.

Now Garth was playing the guitar. I only wished our other friends in Room 26 could have heard him.

When his fingers got tired, Garth decided to clean out my cage. He was very surprised to find the carrot and cauliflower at the bottom of my cage. 'Hey, Humphrey, are you on a diet?' he asked me.

'Be careful,' I warned him. 'They're from the planet Spurling. They may not be safe!'

Luckily, he threw them in the rubbish and examined my food bowl. It was empty, so he knew I'd been eating something.

'I suppose you were just full,' said Garth. 'But I'd better watch what you eat this weekend.'

I could guarantee him I'd eat just about anything, as long as it was from the planet Earth!

That night, I was more awake than usual. Yes, I'm nocturnal, which means I feel a little livelier at night than during the day. But what kept me awake that night was the thought of Og. I could almost picture him boarding the space ship and taking off for Spurling.

I hoped they understood frog language there.

⚬

'It's a beautiful day! We should all go outside,' Garth's mum announced the next morning.

She was right. The Tugwells' garden was a carpet of green grass with red and yellow flowers blooming around the sides. Two-lips, Garth's mother called them.

Garth put my cage on a table on the patio. Garth's dad pushed Andy on a swing at the end of the garden, while Garth's mum dug around in the soil, planting seeds.

'Come on, Humphrey, you need some exercise,' Garth said as he gently took me out of my cage. 'Let's try your hamster ball.'

I would have preferred to run freely in the grass – just like my wild ancestors once did – but at least I had the chance to roll *on* it. The grass looked brighter and greener from inside the yellow plastic.

'Watch him go,' Garth said. His mum, dad and brother gathered around. The sound was a little muffled, but I could hear them laughing.

It was harder to make the ball move on the grass than it had been on the smooth floors of Long-fellow School. The ground wasn't even, and once in a while I'd hit a bump and veer off in an unexpected direction. But I didn't mind because it was fun to explore the garden on my own.

Garth's mum went back to planting seeds and his dad helped her.

'Want to roll!' Andy insisted, so Garth showed Andy how to do a somersault. Then Garth helped Andy get his legs over his head and roll across the lawn.

'Roll, Ham!' Andy called to me. 'Roll!'

So I rolled some more until I hit a hill. It wasn't a big hill, but it was enough of a slope for my ball to pick up speed. Faster. And faster. And a little bit faster.

It was fun! It was exciting!

It was also SCARY-SCARY-SCARY! I stopped walking but the ball kept rolling. I knew that cars slow down when humans step on the brakes.

Unfortunately, hamster balls don't have brakes, so I tried to flatten myself on my tummy, pushing down hard with my paws, hoping that would help slow the ball down.

It didn't. The ball rolled and rolled and rolled some more until it finally came to a stop near some bushes at the back of the garden. Whew.

The ball may have stopped but my head was still spinning. I was tired and a little thirsty, but at least I was safe inside the plastic.

It was nice in the shade. Dark, leafy and quiet. A little too quiet.

I could hear Garth and Andy laughing, but they sounded very far away. And they didn't sound like they were looking for me. I realized that if they didn't miss me, I'd never be able to roll the ball back UP the hill.

I sat there in the ball, catching my breath and hoping to come up with a Plan. I was distracted, however, when a long dark shadow fell over the ball.

I looked up and was shocked to see two beady eyes, a number of huge teeth and some horrible long whiskers, hovering directly over my head!

I recognized the face. It was – oh no – a cat!

'Eeek!' I squeaked.

The face moved in closer to the ball. A long pink tongue poked out from the sharp white teeth.

I might have fainted, but I didn't dare risk it. I needed to stay calm to deal with this crisis, but 'Eeek!' I squealed again. I didn't mean to. It just slipped out.

A huge paw dropped down on top of the ball. BOOM! – I fell flat on my back. Funny how I'd worried all night about Og's safety and here *I* was the one in great danger! (Well, that wasn't so funny after all.)

The cat leaned in closer and opened his mouth wider to show off his pointed teeth, just in case I missed them the first time. He took his paw off the top of the ball. Whew! Maybe he was losing interest.

But no, the next thing he did was lie on the ground with the ball – and me – between his front paws. Then he began a charming little game. He batted the ball from one paw to another, which made me feel like I was in a game I saw at Kirk's house. Pinball, they call it. BOP-BOP-BOP the ball spun from side to side – I spun, too. One second I was upside-down, then I was right side up, and I also slid from side to side. This might have been the cat's idea of a fun game but it wasn't mine, because I was pretty sure I wasn't going to be the winner.

While I was being tossed around, I started wondering how easy it would be for the cat to open the ball and get at me. My cage, after all, has a lock-that-doesn't-lock. What if this hamster ball had a catch-that-doesn't-catch? The catch was . . . I'd be caught!

'Sweetums! Where are you, Sweetums? Time for din-din!' I heard a voice call in the distance. The cat's head suddenly jerked to one side. So this must be the Sweetums who was being called. While he was distracted, I hurled myself against one side of the ball, which then rolled down under a bush.

'Sweetums, Mummy wants her baby girl to come home! Din-din!' the voice called out again.

Oops. Sweetums was a girl. A downright mean one, too.

Sweetums poked her head under the bush and batted at me with her paw. Luckily, the ball was wedged against a branch.

'SWEE-TUMS!' The voice was more insistent. 'Yummy din-din!'

I suppose Sweetums decided that din-din in the dish was more of a sure thing than a hamster in the bush, and she trotted away, leaping over the fence and into the garden behind the Tugwells' house.

I was relieved but I was also a little lonely. And a little thirsty, too.

I suddenly thought that after Sweetums finished her din-din, she might come back to the Tugwells' garden for dessert. Namely me!

Speaking of the Tugwells, where *were* they? They seemed as far away as the planet Spurling.

CAT: Like dogs, cats are extremely dangerous creatures with sharp teeth, gleaming eyes, pointed claws and an appetite for small, cuter animals such as hamsters. If a cat gets hold of a hamster, it can lead to a catastrophe, which I don't even want to think about.

Humphrey's Dictionary of Wonderful Words

The Hunt Continues

The Tugwells were looking for me. They just weren't looking hard enough.

I could hear them in the distance, calling my name and arguing among themselves.

'How could you take your eyes off him?'

'I've looked everywhere!'

'Have you checked those bushes?'

'Of course!'

'We have to find him before dark!'

'Maybe we need some help.'

'Help find Ham!'

I tried to move my ball, but it wouldn't budge. I was stuck.

It was quiet for a while, which made me a little nervous, but I tried to stay very still and rest. I tried not to think about water . . . or Sweetums.

I woke up when I heard big footsteps clomping

through the grass.

Voices called out, 'Humphrey! Hum-phrey!'

And one voice was so loud it was unmistakable, saying 'Humphrey, tell us where you are!'

It had to be A.J.

'I'm HERE-HERE-HERE!' I squeaked as loudly as a hamster can.

I don't think anyone heard me because the voices kept calling.

'Humphrey! Humphrey! Humphrey!'

'HERE-HERE-HERE!'

For some reason, we weren't making any progress.

It was quiet again, and then I heard more footsteps, thudding through the grass.

'Look over there,' a small voice whispered.

'I'm here!' I squeaked.

'How about those bushes?' a second voice asked.

'OVER HERE!' I yelled.

Then I heard it. 'MEEOW!'

I made the mistake of looking up.

Sweetums was poised on top of the fence, staring down at me. Din-din was over. It was time for dessert.

'UNDER THE BUSH!' I yelled at the top of my tiny lungs.

I heard more footsteps crunching on the fresh new grass.

'Down there,' said a voice. 'Ham?'

That, I knew, was Andy.

'I'll crawl under there,' said the other voice.

It seemed like a long time before I saw someone looking right at me. It wasn't Sweetums this time, thank goodness. It was DeeLee, A.J.'s little sister.

'Here's a ball. Oh, it's Humphrey. Come here, sweetie.' DeeLee reached in and grabbed the ball. She was a little rough, but I didn't mind.

'Hi, Humphrey.' She had a big smile on her face. So did I.

'Hi, Ham,' said Andy. I didn't mind being called a ham. I just didn't want to be called 'dessert'.

'Meow!' called Sweetums, obviously jealous of the attention I was getting.

'Hi, pretty kitty,' DeeLee answered.

I cringed at her cat-friendly tone, but I forgave the girl, because she'd saved me.

Carrying the ball (and me), DeeLee raced up into the garden. 'We found him! We found him!' she squealed.

Soon, all of Garth's family and all of A.J.'s family gathered around.

'Well done!' said A.J., hugging his sister.

'Let's get him to his cage,' said Garth's mum. 'He needs food and water.'

She sure got *that* right.

As we all hurried towards the house, I thought about Sweetums and how disappointed she must have been.

Too bad, I thought. I only hoped that Og was as lucky as I was when the aliens came to take him away.

∴

I drank and drank and drank. I know my friends drink fruit juice and lemonade but nothing in the whole wide world tastes better than water. Trust me on that.

Mrs Tugwell served the Thomases lemonade and biscuits, and they all laughed and shared stories about me, Garth and A.J.

'When you rang and asked if A.J. could help look for Humphrey, I said, "We're all going",' Mr Thomas said. 'We had to help our little friend.'

'*I* found him!' DeeLee bragged.

And I was GLAD-GLAD-GLAD she had.

While the families talked, Garth and A.J. stayed unusually quiet.

'Why don't you take A.J. to your room?' Garth's mum asked.

'Okay.' Garth didn't sound very enthusiastic. 'Can we take Humphrey along?'

'Yes,' said Garth's mum. 'But be gentle with him. He's been through a lot today.'

This was a very clever woman.

Once we were in Garth's room, the boys got quiet again.

'It wasn't my idea to ring you,' Garth finally said. 'My dad made me.'

'I'm glad he did. My sister found Humphrey, didn't she?' A.J. replied.

'Along with my brother,' Garth snapped back.

They were quiet again. Under ordinary circumstances, I would have spun on my wheel to entertain them, but I was far too weak.

'What's that?' A.J. asked after a while.

'My guitar,' answered Garth.

'Can you play it?'

'Sure.' Garth took the guitar out of its case, fiddled around with the strings then began to play 'Down in the Valley'.

'Hey, you really can play,' said A.J.

'I said I could.' Garth's voice had an edge to it. He started playing another song.

'I wish I could play.' A.J. sounded wistful. 'Can I try it?'

Garth thrust the guitar at A.J. 'Okay.'

A.J. tried to play, but I have to say it sounded AWFUL-AWFUL-AWFUL! We hamsters have sensitive ears, and mine were hurting from the terrible sounds that came out of the guitar when A.J. tried to play.

He stopped abruptly, thank goodness, and handed the guitar back to Garth.

'Here,' he said. 'I'm no good.'

'Nobody's good in the beginning,' said Garth. 'I've been practising for months.'

He started strumming again and it sounded good.

'We're going home, my boy,' A.J.'s mum poked her head round the door. 'Garth's parents said you can stay if you'd like.'

'Okay,' said A.J.

'Okay with you, Garth?' asked Mrs Thomas.

'Yeah,' Garth answered, but he didn't sound as if he meant it.

After A.J.'s mum left, Garth and A.J. were quiet for a while, which wasn't normal for them. They stared at my cage and finally Garth said, 'Maybe Humphrey's ready for another spin.'

My stomach did a somersault at the thought of meeting up with Sweetums again, but this time he put me in the ball and let me roll around his bedroom floor. I was pretty tired of rolling, but the thought of coming face to face with a cat or a dog or some other dangerous creature had me worried. It was time for me to take charge of my hamster ball!

Garth strummed the guitar but I hardly noticed. I already knew how to make wide turns, but now it was time to try sharp turns. I spun my body to the right as fast as my legs would go, but the ball wobbled rather than moving very far.

A.J. laughed. 'Look at Humphrey Dumpty.'

Garth laughed, too. 'He looks a little seasick.'

Once the ball stopped wobbling, I decided to try again. I remembered once seeing some boys on skateboards on the pavement. They could leap up in the air and land, reversing the direction of their boards. I took a deep breath and leaped up, turning my body at the same time. The only thing that happened was that I hit my head on the ball and did a double somersault, which is a pretty good trick, but not what I was aiming for.

Meanwhile, I heard A.J. ask Garth if he could teach him to play the guitar.

'I'll try,' said Garth. He didn't sound too convinced.

As the boys sat side by side on the bed, Garth showed A.J. where to put his fingers and how to strum the strings.

It still sounded terrible, horrible and very, very bad!

'I'm hopeless,' said A.J.

'You could be good.' Garth sounded a little friendlier. 'Try it again.'

I was already trying again. This time I didn't hit my head and I kept my balance as I leaped to the right. And what do you know? The ball made a faster turn to the right. It was still circular, but I felt more in control.

But A.J.'s guitar playing was way *out* of control.

'I give up.' A.J. handed the guitar back to Garth.

Garth picked out a few notes. 'It sounded terrible when I tried in the beginning, too. You just need practice.'

Suddenly, A.J. jumped up and pointed right at me. 'Hey, look at Humphrey! That's so cool!'

What I was doing was pretty cool, if I do say so myself. First, I made a tight left-hand circle. Then I leaped to the right and did a tight right-hand circle.

Garth and A.J. got down on their knees and watched me. 'That's amazing!' A.J. exclaimed. 'How'd he work that out?'

'I think he was practising,' Garth said. 'Now he could be in the hamster ball Olympics!'

'You know what? You could throw the ball better if you practised,' said A.J. 'Don't you ever play catch with your dad?'

'Dad said he's not very good at playing ball,' Garth told him.

'Oh,' said A.J. Then after a while he added, 'Maybe I could practise with you. You could help me with the guitar and I could help you with softball.'

'You really think I could get better?' Garth asked.

'Of course,' said A.J. 'Look at how good Humphrey is at playing ball!'

And I was very good indeed. Sweetums would have a hard time keeping up with me now.

Garth's dad popped his head in the door. 'We're ordering pizza for supper. You like pepperoni?' he asked A.J.

'Yeah!'

'If you want to spend the night, your mum said she'd drop your clothes off,' Mr Tugwell added.

'Okay with you, Garth?' A.J. asked.

'Okay!'

I was glad to hear that Garth answered without a bit of hesitation.

Garth took me out of the hamster ball and put me back in my cage. While the family ate pizza, I took a long nap, and I dreamed about beautiful guitar music instead of space aliens and cats.

·ö·

The next afternoon, A.J. talked Garth into coming outside. 'We'll just toss the ball around,' he said.

'I won't be good,' Garth warned him.

'Maybe not, but you'll get better than you are now,' A.J. said. 'Just like the guitar. Or the hamster ball.'

I was happy they left me in the house. Although I had a new technique, I wasn't anxious to come nose to nose with Sweetums again. She might still be looking for dessert.

Even though I was inside, I could still hear Garth and A.J. laughing and shouting in the garden.

'Nice catch,' A.J. said once. 'Well done!'

I spun on my wheel with pure joy. Even without a Plan, I'd managed to help my friends. *That* was the best trick I'd learned all day.

> PRACTICE: Doing the same thing over and over again in order to get better at it (and all I can say is, if you play the guitar the way A.J. does, you'd better practise a lot). Practice always pays off, especially when steering a hamster ball.
>
> *Humphrey's Dictionary of*
> *Wonderful Words*

No Surprises

'Well, well, if it isn't Humphrey.' That's what Miss Victoria, the bus driver, said when she picked up Garth and me at the bus stop on Monday morning. 'The best-behaved student on the bus!'

That was NICE-NICE-NICE to hear.

Things went so well between Garth and A.J. over the weekend that they sat next to each other and acted like best friends again.

As the bus approached Longfellow School, my whiskers began twitching and my fur began itching. Would Og be there when I got back? Or had he been whisked away to the faraway planet of Spurling?

I'm happy to say, he was there! Nothing at all had changed in Room 26, thank goodness.

'Greetings, green and faithful friend,' I greeted Og.

'BOING-BOING!' was his response.

Mrs Brisbane walked over to the table by the window where Og and I live. 'Are you guys glad to see each other?' she asked. 'Humphrey, I was afraid Og would miss you over the weekend, so I took him home with me.'

Whew! She saved him from an alien kidnapping and didn't even know it.

'Lucky frog,' I said. 'The Brisbanes don't have a cat.' I told him the whole story about Sweetums.

So there we were, back on the shelf by the window and everything looked completely normal in Room 26. But the events of the past week made me realize how quickly things can change. Fire alarms can jingle-jangle, best friends can become foes and things from outer space can invade.

During the morning break, Mr Morales stuck his head round the door and said, 'Did you bring it?'

'Oh no! I forgot again,' Mrs Brisbane replied.

'Okay. I don't want to nag you. Maybe tomorrow?'

'I'll try,' said Mrs Brisbane and the head moved on.

After he left, Mrs Brisbane said something very surprising: 'It was only a little white lie.' She said it softly to herself but I heard it plainly. A little white lie.

I had no idea what she was talking about, but I'd never heard anything good about a lie. Even more confusing was the fact that Mrs Brisbane would lie at all. She might be sad or even angry, but she was always honest.

I couldn't puzzle over what she had said for long because my friends returned from break. For the first time for a while, Garth came in with a big smile on his face. Tabitha slapped him on the back and said, 'Good catch!' Then A.J. high-fived Garth.

I guess all that practice over the weekend paid off after all and I was GLAD-GLAD-GLAD.

But I didn't feel so happy later in the day. Mrs Brisbane became extremely annoyed when Heidi Hopper blurted out answers – not once, not twice, but three times! (I was a little annoyed with her, too.) If Mrs Brisbane had talked to her parents, it hadn't done any good.

After lunch, Mrs Brisbane announced that we were going to have a surprise guest! That got my brain spinning as fast as my wheel. The surprise guest at Richie's party had been a magician! Or maybe it would be Firefighter Jeff to help us practise Stop-Drop-Roll. (I hoped it would be him.) Just as I was getting excited, I realized that the guest might not be somebody so nice. It could be Mrs Wright and her really loud whistle. Or it could even be a space alien!

I decided to wait in my sleeping hut. A small hamster can't be too careful.

It wasn't long before the mystery was solved and no one was more surprised than Miranda – because the surprise guest turned out to be her father, Mr Golden! I was almost as surprised as she was.

Mrs Brisbane introduced him to the class and said, 'Mr Golden is an accountant. That means he works with numbers all day long. So he volunteered to spend the afternoon helping us with our maths exercises for the exams coming up.'

Mrs Brisbane is perfectly fine at teaching us all about numbers and the things you can do with them, but it was interesting to see how differently he taught from her. He and my friends played a cool quiz game that just happened to use all the maths that would be on the test. Paul, who usually only comes into Room 26 for maths in the morning, joined us for the fun. Even Pay-Attention-Art paid attention and so did I.

I'd had a pretty exciting day and by the time the last bell rang, I was looking forward to a quiet evening and a nice long doze.

Then I remembered the room cleaning. Would Aldo be back? Or would the space alien return? Would she be taking us with her?

I suddenly didn't feel like dozing, not one bit.

'Og? You know what to do?' I asked my friend later that night. It was dark outside and someone would be coming to clean the room any minute.

He splashed around, which I decided meant 'yes.'

I'd used the time wisely since school finished and had come up with a Plan.

I waited, I watched, I wiggled my whiskers.

And then I heard the squeaking of the cleaning trolley.

'Remember,' I told Og, 'if it's Aldo, we yell "Welcome back!" If it's you-know-who, we hide and stay perfectly still.'

As usual, the lights were blinding when they were first switched on, but I made out the silhouette of someone too short to be Aldo. It was HER! I dived down and burrowed under the bedding in my cage, completely covering myself.

Things were quiet from Og's direction so I figured he remembered his part of my scheme, which was to crouch down and hide behind a big rock.

If we both stayed perfectly still, the creature might not notice us and forget all about taking us back to the mother ship.

I could hear her moving chairs around, sweeping, probably dusting, emptying the two waste-paper baskets. I even heard her make that strange, other-worldly sound. Was that music – or vibrating signals from the mother ship?

'Hi,' I heard her say. 'Yeah, still cleaning.'

Then she paused. 'No. Just a few more days. Thursday's the big day for Aldo. Talk later.'

I heard a click. There was more shuffling, then the lights went out and I heard the door close.

She was gone. That was good.

She was moving on soon. That was good, too.

But if Thursday was Aldo's big day, did that mean he was moving on with her? Because that was a VERY-VERY-VERY bad idea.

'DID YOU HEAR THAT?' I asked Og once the coast was clear.

'BOING!' I knew that was a 'yes'.

'Aldo's big day is Thursday,' I told him. 'Does that mean she's taking him to Spurling with her that soon?'

Og didn't answer and I understood. I couldn't answer that question. And I certainly couldn't sleep, not for the rest of the night.

My friends worked hard the rest of the week. In addition to Mr Golden, Sayeh's dad and Tabitha's mum all came in to help the whole class with maths.

While they multiplied and divided, I worried about Aldo and a different problem: Heidi Hopper.

There hadn't been any improvement in her behaviour, but every day she asked Mrs Brisbane if she could PLEASE-PLEASE-PLEASE take me home for the weekend. And every day Mrs Brisbane told her she needed to see some improvement in the hand-raising situation before I could go home with her.

I didn't want Heidi to be disappointed, so I worked on a Plan to help her remember to raise her hand. So far in my notebook I'd written:

A PLAN TO HELP HEIDI
1.

I hadn't thought of one single thing, and I suppose Mrs Brisbane hadn't either.

On Wednesday, tears welled up in Heidi's eyes when Mrs Brisbane told her it wasn't looking good for the weekend.

'I just need a sign that you're trying,' the teacher said. 'Couldn't you raise your hand just once?'

Heidi nodded, but she didn't seem sure she could do it.

Neither was I.

Thinking about Heidi took up a lot of my time during the day, but in the evenings I only had one thing on my mind: the alien. She said Aldo's big day was Thursday. By the time she arrived to clean on Wednesday night, I'd been spinning on my wheel for two hours straight, trying to whirl away my worries.

When she turned on the lights, I dived under my bedding to hide. I'm quite sure Og slipped behind his rock.

I heard the usual sounds of sweeping and waste-paper-basket emptying. Suddenly, there was that strange humming noise. The mother ship was calling!

'Hey, what's happening, Max?' the strange being said in a cheery voice. 'Long time no talk.'

I took a big chance and poked my head out of the bedding.

'Oh, you'll never guess where I am.' The space alien sat in Sayeh's chair and pulled her hood back. Her hair wasn't in a ponytail tonight. It was long and straight.

'Longfellow School! I'm not kidding,' she said. 'I'm cleaning.'

She paused and laughed some more. 'Seriously. I'm helping out my Uncle Aldo.'

Uncle Aldo? Aldo was an *alien's* uncle?

'He cleans here at night and goes to college during the day.' She hesitated. 'Yeah, he wants to be a teacher. But he ran into problems with Spanish. So he's got this huge exam and he's freaked out about it,' she explained. 'He got a tutor to help him study at night. I have this break, so I said I'd help him out.'

'Og?' I asked in a shaky voice. 'Are you getting all this?'

Og dived into the water side of his tank and splashed loudly.

The alien – I mean, Aldo's niece – stopped talking. She adjusted a thing that was hanging on her ear. Maybe she wasn't talking to the mother ship at all. Maybe she was just talking on a phone attached to her ear. What a relief!

'I'm happy to help Uncle Aldo out. He's always been so good to me, taking me to the fair and to bowling, always ready to listen to my problems,' she explained.

Yeah, that sounded like Aldo all right.

'He's the one who encouraged me to apply to medical school at Spurling. Yeah, I start in June.'

She stood up and started to pace around the room as she talked.

'It's really weird to be back at this school. It's the same as when I was here, only different.' She examined the decorations on the noticeboard. 'Everything seems smaller than I remember.' Then she gasped. 'Max, I can't believe it, but this is Mrs Brisbane's class! *I* had Mrs Brisbane! She was awesome! She was my favourite teacher.'

She was staring at a big bunch of cut-out flowers that Mandy had made. It was labelled: 'To Mrs Brisbane.'

'I can't believe I'm in Mrs Brisbane's room,' she repeated. 'She made me believe I could do whatever I set my mind to – even being a doctor.'

She listened for a while and then said, 'Oh my gosh, I'd better get back to work! I'm only halfway done.'

Still talking, she strolled over to my cage, reached into her pocket and pulled out something. I gasped, but then I saw it wasn't a ray gun. It was a piece of broccoli. 'I'm supposed to give the classroom hamster a treat from Uncle Aldo. There's a frog here, too. Uncle Aldo told me to talk to them, but I feel a bit silly doing that. I wish we'd had pets when I was in Mrs Brisbane's class. Anyway, I've got to run. Talk to you later. Bye!' She tapped her ear and stopped talking.

Just when I was beginning to think Aldo's niece was clever, she said she'd feel silly talking to us!

But other than that, I sort of liked her. I wished I knew her name.

Og splashed away. After a while, I decided to eat the broccoli, because Aldo's niece wasn't from outer space after all. Spurling was a place on earth, not some other planet. And the only reason she was going to perform surgery on humans was because – thank goodness – she was going to become a doctor! Best of all, I knew why Aldo hadn't been coming to clean and I was pretty sure he'd be coming back soon.

NIECE: The daughter of your sister or the daughter of your brother, but a niece is always a girl. If Aldo happens to be her uncle, she's not just a niece, she's also nice.

Humphrey's Dictionary of Wonderful Words

10

The Return of Mi Amigo

'Heidi, do you know I really like you?' Mrs Brisbane had kept Heidi in during break. I was expecting another lecture about raising her hand and I think Heidi was, too.

'Not really,' said Heidi.

'Well, I do,' the teacher told her. 'You're clever, you're funny and you're a very good student. I enjoy having you in my class.'

Heidi wrinkled her nose. 'Really?'

'Really,' Mrs Brisbane replied. 'I realize that I have never told you that. I've been too busy getting you to raise your hand.'

'Og, are you listening?' I called to my neighbour.

He splashed in the water gently. He was listening all right.

'That's a shame,' the teacher continued. 'I wish I didn't have to spend so much time on that. But I worry that your teacher next year might not get to know what a wonderful student you are, the way I do. I'd like you to break that habit before you move on. Would you like that?'

Heidi nodded her head.

'I think I've made you very unhappy because you haven't been able to take Humphrey home with you. Is that correct?'

Heidi nodded her head again.

Mrs Brisbane smiled her kindest smile. 'I think this weekend you should take him home. As long as you promise to keep on trying to break that habit.'

Heidi's smile was as wide as her face. 'Oh, thank you!' she exclaimed. 'And I will try! I promise.'

Mrs Brisbane smiled, too.

'Then it's all settled. Would you like to give Humphrey some fresh water and tidy up his cage?'

Of course she did.

'Oh Humphrey, I can't wait till tomorrow so you can come home with me!'

I couldn't wait either. But in the meantime, I had a lot to think about. It was Thursday – Aldo's big day, according to his niece.

Would he pass his Spanish exam? Would he come back to clean Room 26 again? There'd been so many surprises in recent days, I was looking forward to things getting back to normal.

It turned out I'd have to wait a lot longer for that to happen.

***

I was spinning on my wheel after school when Mr Morales came into the classroom again.

'Just checking on that contract, Sue,' he told Mrs Brisbane.

Contract? Was *that* what he wanted from her? I stopped spinning and started listening.

Mrs Brisbane sighed and shook her head. 'I haven't been honest with you. I haven't forgotten the contract. But I haven't signed it yet, either.'

Mr Morales looked worried. 'You *are* coming back next year, aren't you?'

Eeek! The thought of Mrs Brisbane not coming back to Room 26 was unsqueakable!

'I can't imagine not teaching next year. But this is my thirtieth year of teaching and I qualify for full retirement.'

Retirement? I panicked. When you retire, you don't go to work any more.

'But you don't have to retire,' the head said.

'No. It's just, well, Bert.'

Bert was Mrs Brisbane's husband and a thoroughly nice human.

'Bert's had a rough year now that he's not working. I want to be there for him,' she continued.

Bert had had a bad year all right. He'd been in an accident and was in a wheelchair, but he could go FAST-FAST-FAST in it and he seemed pretty happy. He spent most of his time in his garage, making things out of wood.

Mr Morales stood up and started pacing around. In fact, he paced right up to the shelf where Og and I live. 'I understand,' he said softly. 'I just can't imagine Longfellow School without you.'

'Neither can I,' Mrs Brisbane agreed.

They were VERY-VERY-VERY quiet and it was time for me to squeak my mind. 'Neither can I!' I said. 'And Bert Brisbane is doing just fine! Better than your students would do without you.'

'BOING!' Og unexpectedly chimed in.

'Thanks for your support, Og,' I thanked him.

Mr Morales chuckled. 'I think your friends Humphrey and Og want you to stay.'

Even Mrs Brisbane had to smile.

'Take your time, Sue,' the head told her. 'I just want you to know which side I'm on.'

I knew he was on the same side as I was. But would our side win?

Mr Morales left, then Mrs Brisbane left. Og and I had plenty of time to think over what we'd heard.

I looked out at Room 26, at the blackboard full of maths problems and the Spring into Numbers noticeboard and tried *not* to think about Mrs Brisbane . . . but how could I help it?

I crawled into my sleeping hut and tried to imagine Room 26 without Mrs Brisbane. It was pretty hard to do. Of course, Mr Morales wouldn't let us students stay alone in the classroom. He'd have to bring in another teacher.

Suddenly, I *could* imagine Room 26 with another teacher and it wasn't a pretty picture, because the teacher I imagined was Mrs Wright. It wilted my whiskers to think of her blowing her whistle at shy Sayeh to get her to speak up. Pay-Attention-Art Patel would be scared silly if he happened to be daydreaming and Mrs Wright blasted her whistle at him.

And my small, sensitive ears would be aching by the end of a whole day with Mrs Wright in charge. Mrs Brisbane knew how to handle my friends' problems without whistles or shouting or being mean. I started to imagine going home with Mrs Wright on a weekend but it was too terrible to consider.

Then I thought of another possibility. What if Mrs Brisbane took me to her house for ever? As much as I enjoy going to the Brisbanes' home, I couldn't stand the thought of not being a classroom hamster any more. I wouldn't get to visit different homes or meet new families at the weekends. And who would help the students of Room 26 with their problems?

I poked my head out of the sleeping hut and loudly squeaked, 'Og, you and I will have to stop her!'

Og took a long, loud, splashy dive into the water of his tank.

He had a lot of wonderful ways to agree with me.

·ô·

I was still trying not to think about Mrs Brisbane when I heard some wheels squeaking down the corridor, towards Room 26.

By now, I was pretty sure that no space ships were landing on the car park. But I wasn't at all sure just who would be pushing that cleaning trolley.

The door swung open and the lights came on. Naturally, I couldn't see anything for a few seconds.

I held my breath and waited. I didn't have to wait long.

'*Buenas noches, señores,*' a voice boomed out. 'You are looking at one very happy *amigo*. An *amigo* who has a bee-plus!'

The voice was definitely Aldo's. But I still could-n't understand everything he said. I knew he was happy. I knew *amigo* meant friend. But why did he have a bee with him? Bees are annoying, noisy insects. And a huge bee-plus would be even more annoying.

My eyes got used to the light – and oh, it was wonderful to see Aldo in his usual work clothes, his lovely moustache bobbing up and down above his smiling lips. He waved a piece of paper in the air.

'A B-plus! I got a B-plus in my Spanish exam.' He walked right up to my cage and waved the paper at me. 'Okay, okay, I usually get As for most of my tests. But this B-plus makes me very happy because I thought I might fail.'

I couldn't imagine Aldo failing at anything. And now I understood that the B he was talking about was a grade, not a buzzy insect.

'Congratulations, Aldo!' I shouted with unsqueak-able happiness.

Og bounced up and down like the goofy frog he is. 'BOING-BOING-BOING-BOING!' he twanged.

'*Gracias, amigos*,' Aldo answered. Then he looked around Room 26. 'Well, the place looks pretty good. My niece Amy did a fine job. *Muy bueno*!'

'She did,' I answered. 'But I thought she was a space alien and I thought she captured you and I was SO-SO-SO worried!'

Aldo laughed heartily, which made his moustache bounce. 'I think you missed me, Humphrey. And you know what, I missed you, too. But if I'm going to teach in a school some day, I needed to pass a foreign language. So I took some time off to study. And it paid off.'

Then Aldo, who has done some very funny things, such as balancing a broom on one finger, did something even funnier. He began to snap his fingers. Humming a catchy tune, he lifted his arms above his head and began dancing between the desks, tapping his feet wildly.

'Go, Aldo!' I shouted.

'¡Olé!' he shouted.

'¡Olé-Olé-Olé!' I chimed in.

I was so happy to have Aldo back, I forgot that Mrs Brisbane might not come back at all.

At least for a minute I forgot.

CONTRACT: A piece of paper that you sign as a promise that you'll do something, like teach in a school or pay your bills. Signing a contract is a very serious thing and you should think carefully before you sign one. (Except for Mrs Brisbane, who should sign that paper without thinking for one more second!)

Humphrey's Dictionary of
Wonderful Words

11

Hoppin' with Heidi

Some things are not surprises at all. Like the fact that as soon as we got into the car after school on Friday, Heidi asked her mother if Gail could come over to spend the night. Heidi and Gail are BEST-BEST-BEST friends and do just about everything together (except once when they had a *bad* argument).

I wasn't surprised when Mrs. Hopper said 'yes', either, because she's a very nice mum.

As soon as I was comfortably settled in Heidi's room, Gail arrived with her backpack. It wasn't long before the two girls were giggling.

'Let's dress up!' said Heidi.

'Okay,' said Gail.

Heidi opened a big square box and the girls pulled out all kinds of hats and scarves and jewellery. 'Let's be princesses.'

Gail put on a firefighter's hat. It was just like Jeff

Herman's hat, only this one was red. 'Stop, drop, roll!' she shouted.

So I did. I dropped down in my bedding and rolled over three times. The girls didn't notice.

'No, Gail. Find something fancy,' Heidi said. She had a shiny gold crown on her head.

Gail took off the firefighter's hat and poked around in the box. Soon the girls had on all kinds of lacy, frilly things and sparkly jewellery.

After a while, Heidi took off her crown. 'Let's play a game.'

'Okay,' said Gail. 'Let's play . . .'

'Cards!' Heidi interrupted.

Soon the girls were playing a game where they slapped down playing cards really fast. They were having such a good time, I decided to take a little nap.

I woke up when Heidi said, 'I'm tired of this. Let's do something else.'

'I have an idea,' said Gail.

I never found out what Gail's idea was, because Heidi said, 'Time for smoothies,' and raced out of the room. Gail sighed, but she followed her friend.

The girls returned a while later, with glasses full of something that was bright pink and looked delicious.

'Here, Humphrey. I've brought you a treat,' Heidi said. And what a treat it was: a big, juicy strawberry!

'I've brought a treat, too,' said Gail. She pushed a perfect little raspberry through the bars of my cage.

'THANKS-THANKS-THANKS!' I squeaked, which made both girls giggle.

'How about we draw pictures of Humphrey?' Gail suggested. I thought it was a very fine suggestion.

Heidi shook her head. 'Not now. Let's watch the princess movie.'

'Oh, I've seen that a million times,' Gail said.

Heidi grabbed Gail's arm and pulled her towards the door. 'So have I. It'll be fun!'

The girls were out of the room for quite a while, which gave me time to think. They were having a lot of fun, but I'd noticed something odd. No matter what Gail suggested – or tried to suggest – Heidi interrupted her with her own idea. And they always ended up doing whatever Heidi said. I was sure that Heidi didn't mean to be so bossy. In fact, I don't think she even knew she did it. But I was starting to wish that Gail could get her own way for once.

That's when I came up with a Plan. I do like making Plans, so while I nibbled on the strawberry, I thought about what I could do to help Heidi see what she was doing.

I slipped my notebook out of its hiding place behind the mirror and turned to the page that said:

1.

And I started to write.

∴

Much later that night, my notebook was back in its hiding place and the girls were ready for bed. While they were in the bathroom, brushing their teeth, I opened the lock-that-doesn't-lock, quietly slipped out of my cage and hid under Heidi's desk.

The girls were giggling when they came back in. 'I'll take the top,' said Heidi.

'Okay,' said Gail.

Heidi's bed was very unusual, because it was really two beds, with one stacked on top of the other.

Gail was already climbing into the bottom bed when Heidi said, 'We'd better wish Humphrey good night.'

Heidi leaned over my cage and said, 'Good night, little Humphrey.'

What she saw was an empty cage with an open door.

'Humphrey?' she said in a much louder voice. 'Humphrey, where are you?'

From my vantage point under the desk, I could see the look of panic on her face as she twirled in a circle, searching every corner of the room with her eyes.

Gail leaped up. 'He's not there?'

'No, look,' said Heidi. 'He's out of his cage.'

Gail looked frightened, too. 'But I'm sure the door was closed.'

'I know,' Heidi agreed. 'But he's not there! Oh, if anything happens to Humphrey, I'll never forgive myself!'

Gail looked around the room. 'But he has to be in this room.'

Soon, the girls were crawling around the room on their hands and knees, calling my name. Finally, Gail spotted me. 'There he is,' she told Heidi in a loud whisper.

'Whew,' said Heidi. 'I'll get him.' She crawled over to the desk and reached out to grab me, but I was way ahead of her. I skittered away to a spot I'd picked out under the bed.

Heidi looked pretty frustrated. 'Humphrey! Why did you do that?'

I wanted to squeak up and say, 'To help you,' but I stayed quiet.

Gail closed the door to the room. 'I have an idea.'

Heidi jumped up. 'I'll chase him out into the open and you catch him.' She was already crawling to the bed.

'Come on out, Humphrey,' she said.

She swung her arm under the bed. I came out all right, and dashed under the dresser.

'Humphrey!' Heidi sounded irritated. 'Come here!'

'He's not going to listen to you,' said Gail. 'Listen . . .'

But Heidi didn't listen. 'I'll get a cup and catch him in that. Keep an eye on him.'

She raced out of the room. Gail sighed and stared at me. Heidi was back in a flash with a large plastic cup in her hand. 'You chase him out into the open and I'll put the cup over him.'

We played that game for quite a while. Gail chased me out from under the dresser. Heidi tried hard to put that cup over me, but I was too quick and too clever. Each time she thought she was going to be successful, I changed directions. I felt a little sorry for the girls. After all, it was time for bed. But I was determined to carry out my Plan.

Finally, Heidi stamped her foot. 'This isn't working.'

'No,' said Gail. 'But maybe . . .'

Heidi suddenly brightened up. 'Wait – I know! We're doing it all wrong. We should move really slowly and tiptoe up to him, so he doesn't even notice us and then we'll get him into the cup.'

'I don't know . . .' Gail sounded doubtful.

'Try it.' Heidi was already tiptoeing. 'We can't talk at all.'

It was funny watching the girls tiptoe around the room, trying so hard not to make a sound. To make it even more fun, I came out into the open more, so they'd think they could really catch me. Of course, the second Heidi started to lower the cup over me, I darted across the room and under the desk again.

'Bad Humphrey!' Heidi said. I actually felt like a bad little hamster, but I wasn't giving up on my Plan yet.

Heidi flopped down in a chair. 'I give up. Don't *you* have any ideas?'

'Yes,' said Gail. 'I have a very good idea. Come with me.'

Gail left the room and Heidi followed.

When they came back, without a word Heidi moved my cage to the middle of the room. Gail got down on the floor, opened her closed fist and placed something orange on the floor.

I stared out at the floor, trying to work out what was happening. Then I saw it: a luscious, juicy, beautiful little carrot wiggling and waggling across the floor. I'd never seen a vegetable dance around like that before. I shuddered to think it might be an alien carrot – until I noticed that the carrot was attached to a string!

This was my chance. I was longing to get back to the comfort and safety of my cage. Gail and her carrot gave me the perfect excuse to go back home.

I waited a few seconds before I ventured out from under the desk.

'There he is!' Heidi announced in a rather loud voice.

'Sssh!' Gail reminded her.

I stopped in my tracks, then headed straight for the carrot.

Gail pulled on the string, drawing the carrot closer to my open cage door.

She wiggled the string and I skittered towards the carrot. She drew the string closer to the cage and I dutifully followed.

At last, the carrot was at the cage door. She jerked the string and the carrot crossed over the threshold of the open cage door. I followed it and was back home again at last.

'Close it,' Gail said, but Heidi was ahead of her. Bam! The door closed firmly behind me.

'We did it!' Heidi was hopping up and down. Gail jumped up, too, and the girls hugged.

'I wish you'd thought of that a lot sooner,' Heidi told Gail.

'I did,' said Gail. 'You just wouldn't listen to me.'

Heidi stopped hopping and stared at Gail. 'Yes, I would.'

'I tried about a million times,' Gail explained. It

was an exaggeration, but I understood how she felt.

'Heidi, you're my best friend and I have fun with you,' Gail continued. 'But every time I have an idea, you interrupt me and never give me a chance to talk.'

Gail was following my Plan even better than I expected. It was all up to Heidi now.

'I do?' said Heidi.

'Sometimes,' Gail answered. 'A lot of times.'

'I don't mean to,' Heidi said. 'These ideas just pop into my head and I say them. I'm sorry.'

Gail gave Heidi another hug. 'You're still my best friend.'

'And you're mine,' Heidi agreed.

Mrs Hopper knocked on the door and said it was time for the girls to go to sleep. Soon, they were tucked into their beds and the lights were out.

'Tomorrow, let's practise being rock stars,' Heidi said.

'I have an idea,' said Gail.

I held my breath, waiting for Heidi's response. 'What is it?' she asked.

'We could make up a hamster dance,' Gail suggested.

Heidi was quiet for a few seconds. 'That's a great idea,' she said.

I was so happy that Heidi had listened, I did a little hamster dance of my own.

'Quiet, Humphrey,' said Heidi.
And I was.

BEST FRIEND: A SPECIAL-SPECIAL-
SPECIAL friend that you want to
spend a lot of time with. A true best
friend is someone who will tell you the
truth (gently) and help you solve your
problems. A true best friend isn't
necessarily a human. A hamster can
do the job very well.

Humphrey's Dictionary of
Wonderful Words

Testing, Testing . . .

Any hopes I had that Heidi was cured of her problem vanished quickly once we returned to school on Monday morning. As soon as class started, she blurted out something about how great it was to have me at her house. Okay, she raised her hand in the middle of her sentence, but it was a bit too late.

I had helped to solve Heidi's problem with Gail, but that was only Step One.

Step Two would be to get Heidi to remember to raise her hand in class. And just like Garth, A.J. and me, she needed practice.

But I couldn't do anything to help Heidi for a while because Monday and Tuesday were testing days! For months, my classmates had been preparing for these big tests and now it was time. I wasn't sure what to expect, but I finally found out: tests were very quiet periods when no one was supposed to squeak up at all.

No one did, except Heidi, who managed to say 'Mrs Brisbane?' without raising her hand at least twice a day.

Unfortunately, I wasn't given a copy of the test, so I spent most of the week catching up on my sleep. Or *trying* to catch up. Just as I would begin to doze off, troubling thoughts would creep into my mind and wake me up. Thoughts about Ms Mac. I could still see her huge dark eyes, her bouncy curls and her great big smile. But over time, the picture of her was getting a little fuzzy, which was a bit sad. She was the first teacher who surprised me by going away and I wasn't ready for that to happen again with Mrs Brisbane.

I suppose the contract was just a piece of paper, but I saw it as a SCARY-SCARY-SCARY thing. If Mrs Brisbane didn't sign it, what would happen to me?

Then I thought about Mrs Wright and her whistle. Whenever I pictured her, I would shudder and concentrate on coming up with a Plan to make Mrs Brisbane stay.

The only good news during those days was when break came and Garth and A.J. happily raced outside to play together. Garth didn't think

A.J. was a dirty rat any more and neither did I. Another thing that made me HAPPY-HAPPY-HAPPY was that Aldo was back to his old self: happy, laughing and full of life. I wished I could say 'Gracias' to the person who had helped him study for that test! And I also wished I could ask him more about Amy. I tried, but even Aldo couldn't quite make out my squeaks.

I felt for my friends who worked so hard at their tests. It wasn't easy for Sit-Still-Seth to keep from wiggling or for Pay-Attention-Art to keep his eyes on the paper and not stare out of the window. It wasn't easy for Gail not to giggle, Kirk not to joke or Garth not to watch the clock, waiting for the bell to ring.

Even super students like Golden Miranda and Speak-Up-Sayeh chewed on their pencils and sighed a lot while they stared at their papers.

'Why do we have to take these tests, anyway?' Don't-Complain-Mandy Payne grumbled during a break between tests.

'So you can prove what fabulous students you are,' Mrs Brisbane explained. 'I know you'll make this school proud.'

I knew it, too, but it was still hard to work out how somebody could be graded on filling in little bubbles on paper.

Mrs Brisbane, being a good teacher, made sure

my friends took time to stand and stretch and relax between tests. Those moments made me feel good, until I remembered that she still hadn't signed that contract yet and there was a very good chance she'd never teach again.

But on Tuesday afternoon, just before the bell rang, Mrs Brisbane made an announcement.

'The tests are all over and tomorrow I have a big surprise for you!'

My friends cheered. So did I.

After class, Mrs Brisbane gathered up her handbag and her lunch bag. Before she left, she came over to check on Og and me.

'You know, Humphrey, I was hoping maybe you could cure Heidi of not raising her hand,' she said. 'But if I haven't been able to make a difference all year, how can I expect a little hamster to change her in one weekend?'

I had to squeak up. 'I made a lot of progress,' I told her. 'We just have to get her to practise.'

Mrs Brisbane grinned mischievously. 'Sounds like you have an idea! Well, so do I, and you can help! See you tomorrow.'

She left quickly and I hopped on my wheel and spun with delight. Wednesday couldn't come fast enough for me!

My whiskers wiggled with excitement when the morning bell rang and Mrs Brisbane began class.

'You all worked so hard on your tests, I'm very proud of you,' she announced after the bell rang. 'So today we're going to have some fun!'

My friends cheered and I let out an extra-loud squeak. Even Og let out a joyous 'BOING!'

'Let's just call this Wacky Day. Or how about Wacky Wednesday?'

Stop-Giggling-Gail led a chorus of laughter, and Mrs Brisbane explained the rules for the day. First, she gave her desk to Og and me. That's right: she asked Richie and Seth to move Og and me from our places by the window to the top of her desk. 'I'll let them be in charge today.'

I LIKED-LIKED-LIKED that idea.

Then she asked all the students to change seats. 'Get as far away from your usual seat as possible,' she said.

There was quite a commotion as my friends all raced around to switch seats.

Once they were settled, Mrs Brisbane explained the rest of the rules:

* All students who were right-handed should use their left hands to write or draw.

* All students who were left-handed should use their right hands to write or draw.

* Students should blurt out questions and answers, and should *not* raise their hands. If a student accidentally waved his or her hand, the other students were required to jump up, wiggle their arms and legs, and make monkey sounds.

My classmates loved that idea, especially when Mrs Brisbane let them practise their monkey movements. I joined in.

'Look at Humphrey. He's a monkey, too!' Art shouted. (For once, he was paying attention.) My friends loved it, even Mrs Brisbane.

So far, Wacky Wednesday was great and it got wackier as the day wore on.

First, we had the Wrong-Hand Art Contest. Everybody had to use the hand they didn't usually draw with. I tried it and it was HARD-HARD-HARD.

'My baseball player looks like he's from outer space,' Kirk chuckled.

He was making a joke, but I still didn't like to think about aliens.

To squeak the truth, the drawings all looked pretty strange. Tabitha won the contest because it turns out she can use both paws – I mean hands – equally well!

Then there was the Trivia Bee. This wasn't like

the 'bee' Aldo got in his Spanish test. This was a game with two teams. Guess who Mrs Brisbane asked to pick one of the teams? Garth Tugwell, the boy who hated getting picked last. The other team captain was Miranda Golden.

'You go first, Garth,' Mrs Brisbane told him.

Garth looked out at his classmates. His eyes rested on A.J. and I was sure he was going to pick him first. Instead, he turned to Mrs Brisbane and asked, 'Wouldn't it be fairer just to count off?'

Mrs Brisbane had an amused smile on her face as she nodded. 'I think that would be very fair, Garth.'

So the rest of the students called out alternating numbers: one, two, one, two, one, two. All the 'ones' lined up next to Garth. All the 'twos' lined up next to Miranda. The funny thing was that A.J. ended up in Garth's team after all.

Next, Mrs Brisbane asked funny questions, like 'What country did Dracula live in?'

Garth had no trouble answering that one. 'Transylvania.'

As I recall, Dracula is a vampire with sharp teeth, so I hope I never have to go to Transylvania.

Mrs Brisbane turned to Miranda and asked, 'What does the legend say you'll find at the end of a rainbow?'

Miranda correctly answered, 'A pot of gold.'

And so the Trivia Bee continued. Any person who missed the answer had to sit down. The first one was Pay-Attention-Art. I guess he stopped paying attention again.

The next to miss was Mandy. 'Can't I try again?' she begged.

Mrs Brisbane told her to take her seat, but she said it kindly.

On the second round, Mrs Brisbane asked A.J., 'Which weighs more: a ton of feathers or a ton of bricks?'

A.J. quickly answered, 'Bricks.' I think he knew it was wrong as soon as he said it, but it was too late. He had to take his seat while the teacher explained that a ton of feathers and a ton of bricks weigh exactly the same – a ton. She is a very tricky questioner!

'Did you get that one, Og?' I squeaked.

The loud splash I heard made me think that perhaps he'd thought the same thing as A.J. did.

'Sorry,' I heard A.J. tell Garth as he passed by him.

'No problem,' Garth replied.

My friends in Room 26 are pretty clever and it took a long time before Sayeh and Garth were the only ones left standing.

Mrs Brisbane asked Sayeh how many biscuits are in a 'baker's dozen'.

Sayeh, who is hardly ever wrong, answered, 'Twelve.'

'Sorry, that's wrong,' said Mrs Brisbane. 'Garth, do you know the answer?'

Garth took off his glasses and cleaned them with his shirt. Then he put his glasses back on and said, 'Thirteen.'

'That is correct,' Mrs Brisbane said. 'If you answer the next question correctly, you win. What did Prince Charming have to do to wake up Sleeping Beauty?'

Garth grinned. 'Kiss her!' he answered. Then, making a face, he added, 'Yuck!'

And so Garth and his team were the winners of the Trivia Bee. As much as I love Miranda, this time I was happy Garth won. When Miranda high-fived him with a big smile on her face, I knew she was GLAD-GLAD-GLAD, too.

Late in the afternoon, Mrs Brisbane played a Brain Teaser game with our class. She would ask a trick question that had a trick answer. The person who gave the first correct answer would receive a very cool sticker with a riddle on it.

The first question was: 'Why can't a man living in the USA be buried in Canada?'

Sayeh raised her hand first. This was a good thing, because Sayeh is quiet and sometimes doesn't answer at all. But it was also a bad thing, because according to the rules of the day we weren't supposed to raise our hands.

'Class? Sayeh raised her hand,' Mrs Brisbane said. 'What do we do?'

Kirk was the first one to jump up and my other friends followed. I joined in, too, as we made funny monkey sounds and jumped around. Even Mrs Brisbane tried it. Nobody laughed harder than Sayeh.

Once everyone was seated again, Mrs Brisbane repeated the question. Tabitha, Art, Kirk, Heidi and Sayeh all shouted out, but since A.J. had the loudest voice, he was the one I heard. 'Because he's still alive!' his voice boomed out.

'That's correct,' Mrs Brisbane replied. 'You can't bury a person who's still living.'

The next question was just as tricky: 'If you only had one match and you walked into a room where there was a candle, an oil lamp and a wood-burning stove, which one would you light first?'

Voices shouted out and I couldn't understand any of them. Heidi looked very frustrated as she waved her hand in the air. When they saw her, the other students leaped up and did the monkey imitation. Heidi seemed annoyed. 'I *know* the answer but no one can hear me.'

'The candle!' shouted Mandy.

'No, the match,' said Art.

The match was the correct answer, even though I would have voted for the stove. It turns out that you can't light anything else in the room without lighting the match first!

The same thing happened with the next question and the one after that. Heidi couldn't make herself heard. Finally, she stood up. 'Mrs Brisbane, I don't think it's fair because the winner is always the person who's the loudest!'

Mrs Brisbane bit her lip and looked thoughtful. 'Do you think it would be fairer if people raised their hands?'

Heidi nodded. 'Yes, and you could call on the first person to raise her hand.'

'So you agree that by raising our hands, this game would run in a fair and orderly way?' asked the teacher.

'Yes!' Heidi sounded very sure.

'Then maybe tomorrow when we go back to our usual rules, you can remember to raise your hand. Do you think you can, Heidi?'

Heidi's face turned bright pink. 'Yes,' she said, 'I can.'

Brilliant! Mrs Brisbane had shown Heidi why it's important to raise your hand, she'd made it fun and everyone – including me – had helped. When class ended that day, I was convinced that she was the BEST-BEST-BEST teacher in the whole wide world.

I was also convinced that I'd be unsqueakably sad if she left and didn't come back to Room 26.

> WACKY: Crazy, silly, goofy, loony, nutty, wild, and if it's a Wednesday, something that's FUN-FUN-FUN!
>
> *Humphrey's Dictionary of Wonderful Words*

The Big Break

'Og, that was the Wackiest Wednesday ever, wasn't it?' I happily squeaked to Og when we were alone.

'BOING-BOING!' he twanged. I'm sure that meant 'yes'.

'And weren't you HAPPY-HAPPY-HAPPY to see Heidi raise her hand?' I asked him.

All I heard was a huge splash, but it sounded like a happy splash to me.

I was so excited about our amusing day, I jumped on my wheel and spun as fast as I could. When I got tired of that, I spun the wheel the opposite direction for a while. I was tired and happy by the time Aldo came in to clean the room.

'*Hola, amigos*,' he said when he arrived.

I'd thought about it for a while and decided that *hola* meant hello.

'*Hola* right back at you,' I squeaked.

Aldo was cheerier than ever now that his Spanish test was over. He hummed and sang and waltzed his broom across the floor. The nightly show Aldo put on was better than anything I'd seen on television at my friends' houses. When he had finished, he offered me bits of lettuce while he ate his sandwich.

'Well, *amigo*, it's time to say *adios* and move on.' He stood up to arrange his bucket, broom and rags on his cleaning trolley. 'I won't see you for a while. I hope you enjoy your trip, wherever you are going.'

Aldo was saying strange things again! I was so stunned that he was halfway out of the door before I could squeak, 'But I'm not going anywhere!' It was too late for him to hear me. He was gone.

I didn't think I was going anywhere, but Aldo seemed pretty sure.

'The contract!' I told Og. 'If Mrs Brisbane doesn't sign the contract, maybe I'll be going away.'

Og didn't respond. Maybe he was as worried as I was. After all, if I went away, he probably would, too.

As I lay in my sleeping hut that night, I thought about what would happen if Mrs Brisbane didn't come back to Room 26. Maybe I was going to live with the Brisbanes. Maybe I was going back to Pet-O-Rama. Maybe *real* space aliens were coming to take me away. None of those thoughts made me very happy.

At least Aldo had said 'for a while'. I hoped he meant that some day I'd be coming back to Room 26, the place I like best in the world.

'ö'

The next two days, my friends seemed sillier and more excited than usual while I was much more serious. I think Mrs Brisbane was, too, especially when Mr Morales came in during break to remind her about the contract. 'Think it over next week, Sue,' he told her. 'I know you'll make the right decision.'

The right decision would be for her to come back. Because if she wasn't in Room 26, who would think up things like Wacky Wednesday and work out how to help Heidi, just as she's helped all my friends throughout the year?

On Friday, just before my classmates returned from break, I looked up to see Mrs Wright standing in the doorway. Her silver whistle glittered.

'Mrs Brisbane, I just want to say that Garth Tug-well is participating much more in sport now. And his skills are improving.'

'Oh, I'm so glad,' Mrs Brisbane answered.

'However, two of your students came out to break without jackets or sweaters on. It's exactly 65 degrees outside and the rules say that students must wear jackets or sweaters when the temperature is below 70. I'm sure you'll remember that rule from now on.'

'I don't think it's a very good rule,' Mrs Brisbane answered. 'If the children play hard, they'll get overheated, which is just as bad as being cold.'

Mrs Wright did something strange with her eyebrows, bringing them down low over her eyes. I think that's called a scowl. 'If you don't like the rules, then why don't you make a proposal to change them? That's why the head has a suggestions box outside his office.'

'That's a good idea,' Mrs Brisbane said. 'I think I will!'

The bell rang and Mrs Wright left, thank goodness.

'Grrr!' Mrs Brisbane made a fist and pretended to pound her forehead with it. 'Maybe I wouldn't miss this place so much after all!' she said. I think she was talking to herself, but I heard her say it.

'But we'd miss you!' I squeaked. 'You have to stay!'

Mrs Brisbane swung around to face my side of the room. 'Humphrey, I hope you're not agreeing with that woman.'

'NO-NO-NO!' I assured her.

❀

All day long, I kept my eye on Heidi. Once she started to blurt out an answer but I shouted 'Hands please!' and even if she didn't understand my squeaking, she got the message and raised her hand.

When the day was almost over, Mrs Brisbane asked my classmates to clean up their tables and the area around them. 'We'll be gone for a week for the spring holidays,' she said. 'We want to come back to a nice room.'

Spring holidays? Where were *we* going for a whole week?

'Eek!' I squeaked.

Heidi's hand shot up. Goodness me, I was proud. When Mrs Brisbane called on her, she asked, 'Where will Humphrey and Og spend the holiday?'

'Humphrey and Og will be at my house,' the teacher answered. A few kids groaned and she asked what was wrong.

'I wish I could have Humphrey for a whole week,' said Garth.

'Me too,' Miranda agreed.

Knowing that Sweetums could get into Garth's back garden and knowing that Miranda's dangerous dog Clem lived at her house made me VERY-VERY-VERY glad I was going home with Mrs Brisbane.

I knew I'd be safe there and maybe – just maybe – a small hamster with a Plan could convince her to sign that contract and come back to Room 26.

All I needed was that Plan.

'Bert? Are you there?' Mrs Brisbane opened the front door of the house. Bert didn't seem to be around.

'I bet he's in the garage,' she said. She put my cage on the living-room table. 'I'd better bring Og in.'

It was nice to be back at the Brisbanes' house. Next to my cage was a vase of pink and white flowers. Mrs Brisbane always had flowers in her house – real ones. Soon, Og's tank was next to me on the table.

'Nice to be back, eh, Oggy?' I asked my companion.

'BOING!' he twanged.

I do like visiting the Brisbanes, I really do. But the thought of never seeing my friends in Room 26 was still a worry. *If* Mrs Brisbane didn't sign that contract.

Mrs Brisbane left again and when she returned, her husband came in his wheelchair behind her. A smile now replaced the grumpy old frown he had the first time I saw him.

'My two favourite mates!' he exclaimed when he saw us. 'I've missed you.'

'You spend so much time in the garage, you wouldn't know if they were here or not,' Mrs Brisbane said in a teasing way.

'I used to spend my time cooped up in a little box in a big office. I love having that whole garage all to myself,' he said. 'I'll have to show you my latest creation: a three-storey bird box.'

Mr Brisbane liked to make things. The best thing he'd made was my large cage extension, with all kinds of wonderful places to hide, swing and climb.

'I should think you're happy to have a break,' he said to Mrs Brisbane.

'Yes, I am,' she said. 'Especially after today. Ruth Wright complained that I let some children go out without sweaters when it was 18 degrees instead of 20. Is that all school has become: rules about sweaters and fire drills instead of teaching children to learn and grow?'

'It never will be with you around, my dear,' he answered.

'She said I should put my suggestions in the suggestions box. Well, I have a suggestion for her!' Mrs Brisbane was getting pretty heated.

'I suggest you come out and see my bird box,' he said. 'And that afterwards, we order some Chinese food and watch a film.'

Mrs Brisbane gave his cheek a little pinch. 'You're the cleverest man I know,' she said.

Maybe Bert could think of a way to get her to sign the contract.

The next morning, Mrs Brisbane went shopping for new spring clothes. As soon as her car left, Bert came to talk to me.

'Humphrey, I've got to go somewhere and it just occurred to me that it would be a very good idea for you to come along.'

Since I am a hamster in a cage, people hardly ever take me with them when they go out. I've never been to a restaurant, a cinema or a shopping centre. I've never been bowling, skating or camping. Wherever Mr Brisbane was going, I wanted to be with him.

'Let's GO-GO-GO!' I said.

I didn't know where we were GO-GO-GOING but it was fun to be heading out with Mr Brisbane. It took a while for him to get me, his wheelchair and himself into the car, but it was a beautiful day and I was excited to be going somewhere new.

As he was driving, Mr Brisbane said, 'I didn't ask permission to bring you along today, but I'm counting on you to win them over.'

Win them over? When *didn't* I win humans over? I just didn't know which humans he meant. Because if one of them happened to be Mrs

Wright, I'd have to work pretty hard.

Suddenly, the car made a sharp right turn. 'Welcome to Maycrest Manor,' Mr Brisbane said. 'Today we're having a surprise party. And you, Humphrey, are the surprise!'

No one was more surprised than I was.

> BREAK: Another good/bad thing. If you break your arm or a vase, it's a bad thing. But a break at school is like a holiday, and holidays are definitely good things.
>
> *Humphrey's Dictionary of Wonderful Words*

14

A Day at Maycrest Manor

Before we went inside, Mr Brisbane covered my cage with a cloth. 'Just for a few minutes, my friend,' he told me.

Still, I could peep out just enough to see that Maycrest Manor was a huge building with lots of tall windows, plants and trees. Inside I saw people with sticks and walking frames and wheelchairs, and there were other people in colourful uniforms helping them.

'Hi, Bert,' a friendly voice called out. 'What have you got there?'

'Hi, Joyce. This is today's entertainment,' Mr Brisbane answered.

'Great! You can go straight to the recreation room. We'll bring the people in about five minutes.'

We took a lift, which always makes my tummy feel queasy and uneasy, and then we entered a great big room with chairs and tables all around it. Mr Brisbane wheeled us over to a table in the centre and uncovered my cage.

'The people here are all trying to recover from illnesses and injuries so they can go back home again. I was here for a while last year and they helped me a lot,' Mr Brisbane explained. 'Now I want to help them back. All you have to do is be yourself, Humphrey.' As if I could be anybody else!

Soon, the people in uniform helped the people with sticks and walking frames and wheelchairs to come into the room. They all gathered on chairs facing the table. I looked around. I was used to having giggly, wiggly children around me, but these were tired and serious faces.

'Okay, Bert. They're all here,' the woman called Joyce said.

'Good morning,' said Bert in a cheerier than usual voice. 'I've brought you a visitor today. His name is Humphrey. I know how hard you all work at your exercises every day, so I thought maybe you'd like to watch Humphrey work out.'

There was no reaction, just unsmiling faces staring at me from all sides of the table.

Bert had said that I was the entertainment, so I decided to be entertaining. I jumped onto my wheel, just to get things rolling. Then I leaped up onto my tree branch and began to climb. I didn't dare look at the faces around me, but I heard a little commotion. Next, I dropped down onto my bridge ladder and hung from one of the rungs.

Surprise, surprise, I heard chuckles.

'Look at that little fellow!' someone said.

Then I let go and slid down to the floor of my cage. I burrowed into my bedding, and temporarily dropped out of sight of my audience.

'Where did he go?' I heard a voice ask.

'Just watch,' Bert said.

Keeping low to the ground, I tunnelled through the bedding and suddenly popped up on the other side of my cage.

'SURPRISE-SURPRISE-SURPRISE!' I squeaked.

This time people laughed. When I looked at the faces again, many of them were smiling and all of them were leaning in to watch me more closely.

'Of course, Humphrey doesn't always stay in his cage,' Mr Brisbane said. He opened the cage door and put me in my yellow hamster ball. I hadn't even seen him bring it along. 'Sometimes, he likes to go for a walk.'

He gently put me and the ball on the floor. 'Go for it, Humphrey.'

I could see a lot of feet making way for me, so I started walking to propel the ball forward. Since I'd learned how to control my right and left turns,

I decided to zigzag across the room. After a while, I looked back and saw that many of the patients were following me. Some of them were helped by the people in uniform. Some of them were on their own.

'He's over in the corner!' a man in a wheelchair said.

Another man pointed with his stick. 'Look out, here he comes again.'

'If had one of those contraptions, I could go anywhere,' laughed a woman with a walking frame.

It became a fun game of Follow the Leader and I got to be the leader. It was a lovely afternoon and we all had a good workout. Those serious faces looked a little less serious as my new friends wished me goodbye.

When it was time to leave, Joyce was very pleased. 'Bert, can you pop into my office on the way out?' she asked.

That's how I ended up on Joyce's desk while she talked to Mr Brisbane.

'My goodness, didn't that work well! Humphrey got them moving like nobody else,' she said.

'He did the same for me,' Mr Brisbane said.

Then something amazing happened. Joyce offered Mr Brisbane a job as entertainments manager. He'd work for Joyce, who was too busy to come up with new and interesting projects for the patients. And they'd even pay him!

Bert accepted, but said he'd have to talk it over with his wife. He said he was pretty sure she'd be pleased. So was I.

That evening, I was back on the living-room table when Mr Brisbane told Mrs Brisbane the good news. 'I'd really like to go to work every day,' he said. 'And I'd enjoy that work more than I ever liked my old job. What do you think, Sue?'

Mrs Brisbane looked surprised – no, stunned. Then she burst out laughing.

'What's so funny?' Mr Brisbane asked.

'Oh, Bert, I've been trying to work out how to talk to you about this. I still haven't signed my contract for next year.'

Mr Brisbane looked surprised. 'Why not?'

'This is my thirtieth year,' his wife replied. 'I can retire now.'

'Sue! I'm so sorry I didn't realize,' he said. 'Thirty years! We should have a party or something. Do you want to retire?'

Mrs Brisbane sighed. 'I'd miss Room 26 terribly. I'd miss all the wonderful students, especially Humphrey and Og. On the other hand, maybe it's time for someone else to have a chance. Am I really making a difference any more?'

I had to squeak up. 'YES-YES-YES!' I shouted. 'You make a difference every day!'

'Humphrey seems to think so,' Mr Brisbane said. 'And so do I.'

'If I retired now, I'd be the one at home alone all day.' Mrs Brisbane stood up. 'I'm going to think about it for a few more days.'

What was there to think about? Sometimes Mrs Brisbane could be quite frustrating. Sometimes Mrs Brisbane even made me a bit annoyed. But always, Mrs Brisbane was a really great teacher.

Bert spent the rest of the week making plans for his new job. He asked his wife if he could borrow me at the weekends once in a while.

'My students won't like it,' she said. 'But if you tell them it's for a good cause, they might not complain too much.'

They didn't talk about it again for the rest of the weekend, so I spent many a long night spinning on my wheel and wondering what Mrs Brisbane would decide.

On Monday morning, when Mr Morales looked in during break, Mrs Brisbane handed him the contract.

'I've signed it,' she said.

The head smiled. 'That's a great relief. What did Bert think?'

'Bert's got a job and he can't wait to get out of the house,' she said with a laugh. 'It looks like neither of us is going to retire, at least not this year.'

I was so unsqueakably delighted, my heart went THUMP-THUMP-THUMP. Og was splashing so much, he practically created a tsunami in his tank, so I knew he was as happy as I was.

When my friends returned to the classroom, I watched them take their seats. I thought of how I'd watched Mrs Brisbane help Sayeh and Garth, Art and Heidi, Seth, Tabitha, Mandy and Kirk – everyone in the class. Did they realize what she'd done for them?

I was afraid they didn't. I was GLAD-GLAD-GLAD Mrs Brisbane was coming back. And I felt SAD-SAD-SAD that none of us appreciated her as much as we should.

> REHABILITATION CENTRE: A place where people who have been ill or injured go to rest and exercise so that they can get strong again. This process works best when it involves a handsome, creative hamster.
>
> Humphrey's Dictionary of
> Wonderful Words

15

Suggestions and Surprises

'That's what she said, Og,' I told my froggy friend later that evening. 'She wondered if she really made a difference.'

'BOING-BOING!' He sounded truly alarmed.

'I know!' I answered. 'No matter how much I try to tell her that everyone appreciates her, she doesn't understand.'

'BOING-BOING-BOING!' I was so glad that Og seemed to understand.

'If there was just some way to get all her students together to thank her for all she's done! Goodness me, wouldn't she be surprised?'

Og took a huge dive into his tank and splashed noisily.

I remembered what Mr Brisbane had told me on the way to Maycrest Manor. He said they were having a surprise party and that I was the surprise.

'Og, we should give her a surprise party,' I squeaked excitedly. I could just see it! Og splashed like crazy. He wouldn't have any water left if he kept that up.

But how could a tiny hamster and a small frog manage to throw a party?

'*We* wouldn't have to give the party,' I continued. 'If we could just suggest it to somebody like Aldo, or a parent, or Mr Morales.'

Og was silent. Maybe he was thinking. I was thinking, too. I was thinking that Mrs Wright had said that the head had a suggestions box outside his office. If I could just put a suggestion in that box, maybe he would give a surprise party for Mrs Brisbane.

I quickly told Og my idea. His response was quick. 'BOING-BOING-BOING-BOING-BOING!'

'Great!' I answered. 'All I have to do is write the suggestion and take it down to the office.'

The fact that my tiny writing was hard for humans to read, and the fact that I had no idea which office was the head's did not discourage me one little bit.

Now I had a Plan.

⁖

I waited until Aldo had cleaned Room 26 before starting on the note. I neatly chewed a piece of paper from my notebook and took my small pencil. Then, in letters as big I could make them, I carefully wrote:

Suggest: MRS B.
30 YEARS
SURPRISE PARTY

Then I put the note in my mouth and opened the lock-that-doesn't-lock.

'Wish me luck, Oggy. I'm on my way!' I announced.

'BOING-BOING!' I knew that meant 'good luck'.

I then began the longest and most dangerous journey of my lifetime.

Of course, the door to Room 26 was shut. Aldo always closed the door and locked it when he left. How stupid of me not to think of it. I'm not one to give up easily, so I examined the bottom of the door and saw that there was a narrow opening beneath the edge of the door. It wasn't much, but hamsters are able to flatten themselves and slip through some very small spaces, so it was worth a try.

Grasping the paper in my teeth, I crouched down close to the floor and slid under the door. I could feel the bottom of the door scraping my back, but I didn't mind because I'd made it!

It was dark out in the corridor and eerily quiet.

Now I faced another obstacle: which way was the head's office? I knew it was near the main entrance, where I'd been carried in so many times. But the cage was always so thumpy and bumpy, it was hard to see where I was going.

I rushed past the side door to the playground – I certainly didn't want to go *there* at night – to the end of the corridor. The only way to go now was left, so I knew I was going in the right direction. There was some low lighting in the corridor, which made it seem even creepier than if it had been completely dark. The doors here looked like other classrooms, except for a small door that had a sign reading 'Caretaker' over it. Aldo has his own room at Longfellow School? You learn something new every day!

I noticed something else: a sound was following me. *Crinkle-crinkle. Crinkle-crinkle.*

I stopped for a second and the sound stopped, too. I crept forward. *Crinkle-crinkle. Crinkle-crinkle.* The sound was back.

I stopped again and looked back over my shoulder. I couldn't see anything: no Aldo, no aliens, nobody at all. When I turned back, the piece of paper I was holding in my teeth brushed against the floor. *Crinkle-crinkle-crinkle-crinkle*. Whew – that was the sound. I was following myself! I reminded myself to tell Og that part of the story when I got back. But first, I had to find the suggestions box.

I hurried down the corridor, glancing at each door. Then I looked straight ahead. There was the main entrance! And next to it, instead of a normal door, there was a big glass window and an even bigger door than all the other rooms. I moved closer and read the sign over the door: 'Headteacher'.

JOY-JOY-JOY! I scurried as fast as I could towards that wonderful door. All I had to do was to drop my note into the suggestions box and race back to Room 26 for my scheme to be a complete success.

Crinkle-crinkle-crinkle-crinkle. I looked up at that big door but there was no box in front of the head's office! Nothing next to it, either. It simply wasn't there. I stood there feeling completely crushed.

And then I looked straight up. There was a large box attached to the door, way above my head. I backed away so that I could read the writing on it: SUGGESTIONS BOX. That was great, but how was I supposed to get up there? I couldn't climb straight up the side of the doorway because it was completely smooth and there was nothing to hang on to. And even though I'm quite an acrobat, I certainly couldn't jump *that* high.

I remembered once when Richie and Seth made little aeroplanes by folding pieces of paper and throwing them. I wished I'd paid more attention. I considered making an aeroplane out of my suggestion, but I couldn't work out how to fly it up to the box.

Just then, I heard the familiar squeaking of Aldo's cleaning trolley. Normally, I was delighted to see my friend, but this time I didn't want him to find me out of my cage. I dropped my suggestion on the floor and darted across the corridor, into the shadows under a drinking fountain.

Aldo whistled a happy song as he pushed his trolley past the drinking fountain. He didn't notice me, thank goodness. But he stopped in front of the head's office and bent down to pick up the piece of paper. My heart sank when I saw him start to toss it into his rubbish bag. But then he stopped and examined it, lifting the note up so he could get more light.

'*Mamma mia*,' he said. 'Thirty years?' He looked puzzled. But instead of throwing the note into the rubbish, he dropped it into the suggestions box. Then he continued down the corridor, turning right at the corner.

I heard another loud noise: THUMP-THUMP-THUMP. But I wasn't scared this time because I knew it was just the pounding of my heart.

I peeped around the corner just in time to see Aldo lock the door marked 'Caretaker'. He didn't have his trolley any more so I guess he was finished for the night. He wore a hat now and he turned right and disappeared from view.

I counted to one hundred. When I was sure the coast was clear, I raced down the corridor, turned right and slid under the door of Room 26.

Once back, I had to swing back up to my table using the cord from the blinds like a trapeze, but I'd done that many times before. As scary as it was, it couldn't compare to what I'd experienced in the corridors of Longfellow School that night.

'BOING-BOING-BOING-BOING!' Og greeted me.

Once I was back in my cage, I took a long drink of water and caught my breath.

It took most of the rest of the night for me to tell Og all that had happened, and for us both to ponder what Aldo thought about that note and whether Mr Morales would even read it.

•ö•

I spent most of the next day dozing, but once or twice I woke up. I was pleased to see that Heidi Hopper was raising her hand, at least most of the time. When the last bell rang, Mrs Brisbane quietly congratulated her and gave her a riddle sticker.

The rest of the week was QUIET-QUIET-QUIET. After all the testing, and all the silliness, it was nice to be back to a normal classroom, but I was worried. Had Mr Morales got the suggestion? Did he like the idea? And what would he do about it? In my time at Longfellow School, I've noticed that humans can be clever, nice and even important like the head, and still not understand the simplest thing a hamster tries to tell them.

You can have a great idea, you can have a Plan, but sometimes it doesn't work out. Maybe I could think of another way to tell Mrs Brisbane what a great teacher she is, but for now I was fresh out of ideas.

·☼·

Two weeks later, on a Friday afternoon, Mrs Brisbane read aloud to us, which is something she does so well. This was a thumping good story about a pig. I've never seen a pig, but this story made me care about him a great deal. In fact, I was so nervous about what would happen to that pig, I hopped on my wheel for a good fast spin.

Then it happened. That unbelievably loud BEEP-BEEP-BEEP was back and I was so surprised, I tumbled off my wheel into my soft bedding.

'Class, it's the fire bell,' said Mrs Brisbane. She seemed a bit nervous. 'Please form two lines.'

Even though Jeff Herman had said to leave the pets and let the firefighters rescue them, Garth and A.J. took Og's tank, while Miranda gently picked up my cage. Sayeh came forward to help her.

'Children, no!' Mrs Brisbane said.

'Please?' asked Miranda. We were already at the door.

Mrs Brisbane shook her head. 'Oh, go ahead.'

Before I knew it, we were out in the corridor, where all the other classes were lining up. In the distance, I heard the screech of Mrs Wright's whistle.

And then we were outside. It was such a beautiful day! I was hoping there wasn't a real fire, not here or anywhere. But if there was, I was prepared to STOP-DROP-ROLL. As I looked around, I noticed that the playground looked a lot different from the last time we had a fire drill.

For one thing, there was a big shiny fire engine parked near the swings. Sitting on top of the fire engine was our old friend Jeff Herman, smiling broadly. A small stage had been set up with a microphone. Sitting on the stage was none other than Mr Brisbane, in his wheelchair. He was smiling, too. There were all kinds of familiar faces. Was that Aldo? And his wife Maria? Many of my friends' parents were there. And some people who didn't seem to belong there at all, like Joyce from Maycrest Manor and Aldo's niece Amy.

WHAT-WHAT-WHAT was going on? I won-dered. And then I saw a banner draped above the stage. It said: MRS BRISBANE APPRECIATION DAY.

I glanced over at my teacher. I've seen Mrs Brisbane look happy, sad, annoyed, tired, puzzled and even discouraged. But I've never seen her look so surprised.

Mr Morales stepped up on stage and tapped the microphone. 'Ladies and gentlemen, students, we are gathered here to honour one of Longfellow School's greatest assets: Mrs Sue Brisbane of Room 26. For thirty years, she's been informing, support-ing and inspiring students in our community. And I think it's time that we all said thank you!'

The crowd cheered wildly. 'THANKS-THANKS-THANKS!' I shouted as loudly as my little lungs would let me. I heard an enthusiastic 'BOING-BOING-BOING' behind me.

The head continued. 'As we all know, it's not easy to get Mrs Brisbane out of her classroom, so I want to thank Jeff Herman of the fire brigade for helping us arrange this fire drill as part of our scheme. Thanks, Jeff.'

After more applause, Mrs Brisbane was called up to the stage, where she took a seat next to Mr Brisbane, who just couldn't stop smiling. Then, one by one, people came up to the microphone to thank Mrs Brisbane. Aldo said she'd inspired him to go back to college to be a teacher. Amy said she'd inspired her to become a doctor. Joyce said Mrs Brisbane had realized her son had a hearing problem and had got him help. Other parents thanked her. And then, the students of Room 26 were called up to the stage.

Miranda brought me along and Richie and Kirk brought Og, too. Mrs Wright stood in front of the stage and blew her whistle (of course). Garth started strumming his guitar (where did that come from?). Then my friends began to sing a song that sounded a lot like 'Yankee Doodle Came to Town', but with different words.

> Mrs Brisbane came to school,
> To teach us to be smarter.
> When we tried to mess around,
> She made us work much harder.
>
> Mrs Brisbane, keep it up,
> You are oh so handy,
> Keep on teaching kids like us,
> And we will all be dandy.
>
> Mrs Brisbane taught us well,
> Starting in September,
> We have learned so much from her,
> And we will all remember.

Mrs Brisbane, thanks a lot,
We will not forget you,
Don't stop helping kids like us,
For we will never let you.

And then they all shouted, 'Thanks, Mrs Brisbane!'

Mr Brisbane handed his wife a handkerchief and she wiped her eyes. I wished I'd had a handkerchief, too.

Mr Morales came to the microphone again and thanked Mrs Wright. 'It took some clever planning to keep this party and this song a surprise,' he said. 'Mrs Wright taught the children the song during PE. Our classroom volunteers, Mrs Hopper and Mrs Patel, made a lot of phone-calls and our caretaker, Aldo Amato, and his wife helped to organize this day.'

It was nice to think that Mr Morales had made a Plan, too. I always knew he was a very clever human.

Everyone applauded again. But Mr Morales wasn't finished. 'Most of the time, we don't thank our teachers until they retire. I'm so glad we had the chance to thank Mrs Brisbane for *not* retiring. We hope she'll be here another thirty years.'

'At least!' I squeaked, which made Miranda giggle.

'Finally, I can't take credit for thinking of this surprise party,' Mr Morales continued. 'I have to thank the unknown person who left the suggestion in my suggestions box. Thank you, whoever you are.'

'You're welcome,' I squeaked softly.

'So things worked out, Og,' I said that evening when my friend and I were alone.

Og leaped up and dived down into his tank with a gigantic splash. That meant he was happy. So was I.

Sometimes you have to give a Plan a long time to work.

Sometimes things work out differently from what you expected, but they still work out.

Life is full of surprises. And I think that's a VERY-VERY-VERY good thing.

> SUGGESTION: An idea you offer to someone else in order to be helpful. It's a good idea to listen to suggestions, especially if they involve parties and more importantly, if they involve *parties honouring friends* you REALLY-REALLY-REALLY like. If those parties include your favourite humans and nice speeches and some singing, so much the better.
>
> *Humphrey's Dictionary of*
> *Wonderful Words*

·ö·

Humphrey's Top Ten Good Surprises

1 Share something with a friend: like ice cream (or broccoli – yum!) or a great book.
2 Put a note saying something nice about someone on his or her desk. Don't sign it! (And don't use the word 'rat' in the note – NO-NO-NO! Unless you're talking about a pet rat you love. Because pet rats are almost as nice as hamsters.)
3 Throw a surprise party for someone special.
4 Help somebody (like your mum or dad or teacher) without being asked. Now *that's* a nice surprise!
5 Visit someone in hospital or a retirement home. Bring something you can do together, like a puzzle or music to listen to.

6 Offer to read to your younger
brothers and sisters. Or offer to
play a game with them.

7 Draw a picture of someone you like
and give it to that person.

8 Give your dog or cat (or hamster) a
good scratching. They'll like it – but
be gentle!

9 Smile at someone when they least
expect it.

10 Invite a friend over to play with your
hamster. FUN-FUN-FUN!